An Alaskan Love Affair

A Legend of Gold, True Love

and of Alaskan Adventure

Leon Crandell

ISBN: 978-1-958772-76-8

Dedication

Dedicated to my grandchildren:

Tanner, Aubrie, Cashus, Miles, Asher, Hazel, and Weston, whom I love very much and wish a fruitful life with many adventures, little to no drama, and enormous success in life.

Life is like a video game. Recognize the patterns in your hero's journey, understand your weaknesses and strengths, and the fact that history is cyclical - life repeats itself. You will make mistakes but remember that pain plus reflection equals progress. The game of life is a process on loop. Codify the lessons of the past to deal with the future. Know your mind and win the game.

Make your life ark the best it can be. Make your work and passion one and one of your life goals. Feel the pull of your passion, feed it until you are an expert in it, and let everything else be hobbies. And consider the money part; money will get you freedom and choice, maximize your learning, and success will follow.

Success in life is a five-step process.

Step 1.) Have a vision of what you want your life to be like, set goals, and write them down.

Step 2.) Understand your problems and obstacles to reaching your life goals. Alcohol use is a life changer; it's best never to introduce it to the life equation.

Step 3.) Pursue your passion, and work well with others.

Step 4.) Design a way to work around obstacles you will encounter to reach your goals.

Step 5.) Implement your plan, and you'll move in the direction of your vision.

And don't forget to have fun and adventure along the way. Love is the answer to all life's problems.

You only have one go-round at this life.

Make the best of it.

Disclaimer

This book is intended for entertainment purposes only. Any similarities to real people, either dead or alive, are purely coincidental. The legend is the brainchild of the author and is not real or intended to offend anyone.

Although some woke individuals may be offended, the author doesn't give a damn.

My hope is that you, the readers, will become immersed in the adventure, become a fly on the wall, a bird in the sky, a freckle on Tanner's face, or a pinecone on a tree. A book can be better than a movie and a source with which you can let your mind run wild. Switch it up and have fun. Come along for the ride.

Heads-up

This book was originally a screenplay by the same name. The purpose of turning the screenplay into a book is because it has a great story being pushed to a chilling conclusion – a totally made-up legend, a true and lasting love story, and a good amount of Alaskan adventure, it has great content and adventure that young people probably won't get to experience but should not be lost to time, and it would make a great movie.

But, trying to find a movie producer to read the screenplay is a process that comes with a ton of competition from scores of screenwriters. So, publishing a book is the next best thing and something I have experience with. With that said,

If you know a producer looking for a good screenplay to make into a movie, get this book into his or her hands. And I will totally make it worth your while with a 10% finder's fee.

Contact: Leon Crandell at 208 634-6475 or eMail:tleonc@gmail.com

I've written a self-published book, an autobiography, which is a screenplay in its own right, titled: Victory through Fire. And I have another screenplay waiting to make it to the screen, "Bitterroot Experience."

All of my works are available in their entirety upon request.

A Hard Lesson to Learn

Alcohol consumption/abuse invites evil spirits into your life, is a game-changer, and is injurious to your health and future. Marijuana, on the other hand, is not as harmful as politicians and their cohorts and the mainstream media lead people to believe.

However, young people should not abuse it because it can severely impact brain development, which is not fully developed until the age of 25.

Notwithstanding, marijuana is not as harmful to young brains, futures, and society as alcohol is.

To all young people, my hope is that you have many fun-filled adventures and build many great memories to cherish forever. Choose life. Life is short.

CONTENTS

About the Author

I'm a 66-year-old White Mexican/American male, somewhat of an adventurer. I grew up in the California Bay Area in the early and mid-'70s. Then moved to Alaska in 1976, lived there for fifteen years, and now reside in Coeur d' Alene, Idaho.

The story has a lot of similarities to my own encounters, but I also take some creative liberties.

If you enjoy this story, I'm sure you will enjoy reading my self-published autobiography, "Victory Through Fire," available only through me. Reach out to me, and I will send you a signed copy for $12.95. The best 12.95 you will ever spend. Not really, but a great read, nevertheless.

The book is another adventure. An adventure of me riding my 18-speed mountain bike for 358 miles through Alaska in 1987, from Anchorage to Fairbanks, AK.

I have nothing but time to think, so I journey into my past, talk about my growing years, my building construction career, and my accident, as I'm taking on the events of the bike trek. Two stories in one. An adventurer's eye opener that young people and not-so-young people will love.

Chapter 0

Prelude to the Story

From the ominous blackness, we see a spotlight coming out of the night sky and hear the sound of a helicopter. Moments later, there appears on the horizon of a snowfield before the pilot's gaze, emergency warning flairs burning, letting the pilot know where to land to pick up Tanner.

Tanner McKenzie, 40, the protagonist of our story, had just survived a grueling gold rescue expedition where he and his 3 buddies had just climbed Alaska's second-highest mountain, Wrangell - St. Elias Mt., in the winter, where temperatures fell to -110 degrees and where three climbers lost their lives in a bloody shoot out.

The rescue crew loads three dead climbers from the other group into body bags and then into the net platform outside for easy access.

Minutes later, with urgency to get out of the freezing blowing cold, the helicopter leaves the mountain's rescue site and heads to Providence hospital in Anchorage, about 2.5 hours away.

Now minutes away, the pilot says, "Breaker, breaker 10-42, coming in for a landing in 2, we have an alive one, but he's bad. Please advise. Over."

On the other end of the radio, a voice responded, "We have nurses on the ground, waiting to take him into the emergency room. Over."

A few minutes later, the helicopter touched down on the helipad on the hospital roof. The rotor blades swirled as the cold wind blew, and the nurses waited patiently with a gurney.

Tanner was taken off the helicopter and moved to a different gurney by a crew of 6 hospital personnel. Once they had secured him to the new gurney, they rushed him inside.

Tanner fell in and out of consciousness, only remembering bits and pieces. Finally, he remembered the shootout, now being in the elevator; oxygen tubes hanging over his almost lifeless body as he continued to drift in and out of consciousness.

An orderly looked at Tanner, who was awake now, and consoled him, "Hold on, you're at the hospital now."

"Where's my wife? I want to see her," Tanner whispered.

"She's here in the hospital and has been waiting for you for a while. She seems like she is your biggest fan," said the orderly, trying to distract Tanner from the pain he was feeling in his leg.

They left the elevator and went down a long dark hall, entering the operating room where the doctors were waiting to tend to him. They quickly assessed his body and mental state to determine if he could comprehend the situation and the decisions that needed to be made.

The doctor came over to him, looked at him, and said, "This isn't going to be pleasant, but we are going to have to amputate your toes, or you'll lose your entire foot and possibly even your leg."

Tanner cringed at the idea of not having a leg and said, "Go for it, doc, do what you have to do."

"I'll have my nurse send your wife the consent forms, and we'll get started ASAP," the doctor said.

Anxiety and fear chased Tanner. In his thoughts, he saw the lights above him in the operating room blurring his vision, and he began to lose consciousness again.

The doctors loaded him with painkillers and did what was necessary.

"I'm glad that is over. Now I'm going to get that sleep I've been promising myself," he said as he glanced at his nurses.

***

Tanner was still unconscious and being cleaned up before

the nurses took him to his room to rest. Angie, his wife of nineteen years, drop-dead gorgeous, and a well-established geologist, who was tops in the field of gold mining, was waiting in the waiting room until she could speak to the doctor.

Leaning back on an uncomfortable hospital chair, she was tapping her foot on the floor and biting her nails. She stared at the door, waiting for news. The doctor finally walked in and up to her.

Angie stood up and asked, "How is he?"

"He's going to be all right, I wish we could have saved those toes on his foot, but he is one of the luckiest sons of guns I've worked on in years," the doctor said, smiling at Angie.

She sighed in relief, knowing that her husband was still alive and breathing.

Tanner McKenzie lay in his hospital bed as his eyes opened, the sun coming through the half-opened blinds. Feeling woozy, he stared at the ceiling taking a few deep breaths before Angie walked in, making her way from the waiting room.

"Hey baby, I missed you," she said as she smiled.

"I missed you more, my love. How long have I been out?" he asked as he cleared his throat.

"A day and a half, and you probably don't remember what

today is," she said, holding eye contact. He shifted in his bed, knowing exactly what she was talking about.

"Hmm, I wonder what today is, sweetheart, I wonder," he said with sarcasm.

Tanner and Angie stared at each other; they both felt grateful for him being alive after the shootout on the mountain.

Celebrating his 41st birthday in the hospital, five of his close friends came to see him. Angie sat on a chair next to him, and Ken sat across from Tanner's bed. One of his Alaskan buddies, Michael, stood by the door, and a few hiker friends that Tanner had met after coming to Alaska were there too.

"That was a close one, bud. Glad you decided to stick around," Michael said.

Angie laughed and looked at Tanner, "Yeah, I'm not finished with you yet."

"Well, I can't figure out if I love you, Alaska, or the gold more," he said with a joking tone in his voice.

Angie squinted her eyes with a deadpan expression. Tanner looked at her and said, "Just kidding love. Without you, my life would be meaningless."

After a few moments of silence, Michael cleared his throat and said, "So, you almost met your maker, I hear. Why don't you light those candles and make a wish?"

He pointed to the cake set in front of Tanner.

Tanner looked up at Michael and smiled, knowing exactly what he'd been waiting for.

"I've been waiting to eat some cake for half an hour. Then, you can tell us the gory details," Michael said, staring him down.

Angie lit the candles on the cake and looked at Tanner. He closed his eyes, and instead of making a wish, he thanked God for this incredible journey called Alaska.

Tanner had just come through the most horrific ordeal of his life. He blew out the candles and said,

"Okay, now pay attention because I'm only telling the story once tonight."

Then a dreamy transition, and the story begins.

Chapter 1

In the Beginning

Tanner, 19 and in his first semester of college, stood in the driveway of his multimillion-dollar home situated in Burlingame, California, surrounded by homes and hills.

His two-story house had a 9' tall, golden brown, and beautifully carved front door with stained glass windows on the sides and top of it.

Tanner's home was the biggest in the area. Evergreen fir trees surrounded the house. The lawn took up a large portion of the hill it sat on, making it feel like the holidays were constantly being celebrated at their house.

The garage next to the house seemed big enough to be a house on its own. This was where Tanner kept his climbing gear and the spot he and Ken hung out and planned their next great adventure.

Tanner's light blond hair was 15" long and fell past his shoulders. Talking to Ken, his high school buddy, one sunny day in May of "76" as he did some touch-ups on his little homemade dovetail trailer, they discussed plans for the summer.

Ken was quite a good-looking young man with wavy brown hair a few inches down his back, an athletic adventure seeker, and a rock climber too.

Ken spoke to Tanner as Tanner made the touch-ups on the little trailer. Ken, kneeling on one leg, indifferent to his clothes getting dirty, stood across from Tanner, helping him polish his new "76" blazer.

"I'm sure glad I made the time to make this trailer in my woodshop class," Tanner said to Ken feeling quite content with himself as he did his work.

Tanner, lost in thought, came back to reality and continued speaking,

"It's hard to believe that I've had this for four years now.

Ken looked at Tanner and said, "I've always thought that this was the nicest trailer around."

"Did I tell you that my mother went to Alaska this summer to see some guy she met at her work? She said that "*'the Alaska Pipeline is being built,'* And that I ought to go up there and check it out."

"Maybe you can find some work for the summer," she said.

Tanner continued his work and then said, "You know Angie is still up there, right? I want to go up there and be with her for the summer, but this time I want to go up into the interior and see more of Alaska's beauty."

He continued to paint on his trailer and got lost in his thoughts again. After a while, he put down his paintbrush and walked to stretch his legs.

***

As he walked away, Tanner began thinking about last summer with Angie.

Chilling on the ferry's deck, Tanner and Angie were separated by distance but always in love. He pictured them in front of one another in a warm embrace on the ferry's deck.

Angie was in her costume, ready to go as the last whistle blew for departure. In Skagway, Alaska, she landed a job working as a dance hall girl in the tourist attraction "Soapy Smith and his Dance Hall Girls."

"I wish you'd stay with me, Tanner," she said as tears formed in her eyes.

"You know this is something I have to do," replied Tanner staring into her eyes. He wiped the tears running down her face.

"I understand, babe. Go, but remember, you are the love of my life and always will be. I'll be waiting right here for you," she said to him as she hugged him tightly.

"You are the only woman I'll ever love. I'll be thinking of you every minute we're apart," Tanner whispered to her as he hugged her back, getting one last whiff of her hair before they parted ways for the winter.

***

Tanner walked back toward Ken as he zoned back to reality, still thinking about Angie. Of course, he thought about Angie most of the time, but somehow this time, it was different.

He sat back down to finish his trailer, sighed, and looked at Ken with a faint smile.

"The ferry took us from Seattle up the inside passage; we went to Ketchikan, Wrangell, Juneau, Sitka, and other stops along the way. Then to Skagway, which is where she is now," he said as he began working on the inside of his 76" Blazer.

Tanner smiled to himself as he continued working on his car. He looked back up at Ken with a big smile on his face as he began to babble on.

"You would not believe the scenery and wildlife we saw just from the ferry. We saw glaciers, bears, eagles, and whales jumping."

Tanner continued expressing his experience when he was with Angie in Alaska last summer.

"When we stopped in the ports like Wrangell and Sitka, we saw totem poles and incredible Ivory carvings. Little kids surrounded us when we were ready to catch the next ferry going North in Wrangell. They were selling garnets they dove for in the Stikine River. So, we bought a bunch of really beautiful ruby red and green garnet stones."

Just as Tanner finished talking, he imagined the kids surrounding him and Angie at the ferry dock, and his smile began to fade.

He returned to buffing out the coat of wax he put on his blazer, which they would use to tow the dove trail trailer. Looking at his reflection on the shiny blue coat of paint, Tanner inhaled and said, "But when I go up there this time, I probably won't be coming back."

He looked up at Ken and grinned at him as he finished speaking. Ken nodded; he understood exactly where Tanner was "coming from."

They stepped inside the house through the back door and straight into the large kitchen. Tanner's mother loved the retro style, so she made sure the kitchen had a retro feel to it.

A small stained-glass chandelier was placed in the center of the kitchen with a yellow bulb; it illuminated the entire kitchen giving the room quite a retro ambiance.

Everything in the kitchen was made from natural oak wood, including the cabinets, drawers, and the large counter at the end of the kitchen, which connected the kitchen to the living room.

Tanner walked toward the sky blue-colored counter; the countertops were the only part of the kitchen that differed from the oak wood's natural light brown tint. He moved a vase and some crockery out of the way, unfolded, and placed a map on the counter. They were making plans for their future.

"If we go straight up the highway, we can cross into Canada right here, take the ferry up the inside passage, get off in Skagway where Angie is, cross the inlet in another ferry, go back into Canada, and then back into Alaska right here, in Tok junction," Tanner said as he pointed at specific places on the map and then looked up at Ken.

Ken stared back at him with bewilderment, as though he wanted to ask Tanner a question.

"What?" Tanner asked.

Ken looked over at the dog, then back to Tanner, and asked, "Are you taking the King?"

Tanner hit his forehead at the question, and with a big smile on his face, he said, "Of course, he's my climbing buddy, my child, and responsibility for life."

Chapter 2

Into the Unknown

Ever since his grandfather made a bundle in the stock market, the McKenzie family had belonged to extreme wealth and luxury. Tanner grew up living like a little prince. Shortly after Tanner was born, his father started his car dealership.

Tanner's dad now owned a 500-car dealership called Good Toyota, and unlike his father, Tanner had an obsession with photography, nature, and rock climbing.

The dealership was big and spacious, the large parking lot was designed, and cars were set and staged to look beautiful. There was a big one-story building that held five to eight cars inside, offices for employees, and the boss's office.

Don McKenzie sat in his big office with wall-sized windows that let in a tremendous amount of light. Inside his office, his award plaques covered the walls.

Tanner walked into the dealership with both his hands stuffed in his hoodie pockets as his thick blond hair bounced to the sound of the music coming from his headphones. Walking into the building, he looked at the cars, employees, and customers engaging with one another. Then, he stepped into his father's office as his dad tilted his head up and looked at him.

"Have a seat, son," Don said. Tanner took a seat across from his father and smiled at him.

"What's up, dad?" Tanner asked with his hands still in his hoodie pockets.

"Your mother and I would like to talk to you tonight at dinner. It's about your plans after college," he said seriously as he and Tanner looked at each other.

"I'd like to talk to you and mom at dinner too, big guy," he said, smiling.

Don, nodding, squinted his eyes at his response with a little suspicion and said, "Okay then."

***

At the dinner table that evening, everyone sat down for dinner. Tanner's mother had had their chef come in. He had prepared a wonderful meal consisting of a chicken alfredo sauce with pasta, a beautiful, fresh salad, and a baguette with a creamy garlic spread.

Sitting around the rectangular 20-setting dinner table, Tanner dug into the scrumptious meal. Finishing the food in his mouth, he was getting ready to say something to his parents.

"Ken, Jon, and I were talking about going to Alaska again for the summer. We'll be coming back in time for the new semester if we go. But I might just stay this time too. I haven't made up my mind yet," he said and then looked at his parents for their reaction.

Don looked up at him with his eyebrows raised and said, "I was hoping you would work at the dealership this summer."

"I told you before, dad. The dealership is your thing. You know I've been pursuing wildlife photography as a career, and Alaska is the perfect place for great wildlife photos," Tanner said, emphasizing his words.

Everyone continued to eat, Don was quietly thinking to himself as if he were preparing to say something, and finally, he did.

Don looked up at Tanner, fork in hand, and said, "You know I'm going to be retiring soon. So you have the perfect opportunity right here to step into my shoes if you want," he said as he refreshed his cocktail.

Tanner stayed silent, still looking at his father, waiting for him to finish speaking as he sighed.

"Alright, son, that's how I know you're my kid because I had that same adventurous spirit at your age, and I had to go out to make it or break on my terms. So go, you have my blessing."

Tanner sighed again with relief and then looked at his mother, Wanda, who had a surprised yet upset look on her face.

"You mean that you want to leave me in this big house alone? What am I going to do with myself?" she said in a sarcastic tone, but deep down was much more serious, followed by a joke. "Maybe I'll start selling cars too."

Don raised an eyebrow. Wanda put her fork down and sighed too.

"I guess if you've got to go, you got to go," she said, looking at Tanner.

Tanner nodded at his mother in acknowledgment and then turned to his father.

"You know, dad, the pipeline is almost complete; there are so many construction jobs up there right now. They say that Alaska is the place to be for the next twenty years or so, especially for young families. And you know Angie and I have been talking about getting married."

Tanner looked at his mother and father once he finished talking, and a smile appeared on his face.

Don nodded, "That is one special girl, I must say."

Wanda added to the conversation, "I really like that girl. She is so smart and pretty and very good for you, Tanner."

“You’re going up there to chase after that gold, aren’t you, son?

It’s no legend. I loaded the gold myself. I remember it like it was yesterday.”

Tanner remembered his father talking about it before. “Tell me more about it, dad.”

Don didn’t have to be asked twice. He began telling the story again.

“It was a cold and rainy night, and the troops were gathered outside the tent waiting for the next command. I told my general, *“The gold is ready to be loaded, sir,”* and he looked at me and said, *“Well, what are you waiting for, soldier?”*

I smiled at him, *“We are waiting for the final command from our fearless leader, SIR.”* He was not amused. He stared at me with a stern look on his face, after which I told him we’d get started right away.

I was a sergeant at the time. I left the tent, took a few men with me, and marched away. We arrived at a B-52 cargo plane a few hundred feet from the tent where the gold was waiting to be loaded.

The men looked at me as I said to them, *“You heard the general. Let's make short order of it.”* We loaded the gold and went back to our barracks.

Don came back to reality as he finished telling his story.

"Fact is, it was almost 6 million dollars' worth of gold bars that went down in the mountains, between Alaska and the Yukon Territory in 1941, is the best we can guess from the last time we had contact with the plane," he said as Tanner looked at him. Don glanced down at the table and then looked up.

"The US Government was paying off the Russians to help us fight the Japanese, days before the invasion on Pearl Harbor, in November 1941. We loaded around 400 bars, and each one was worth about $14,000 a bar. You do the math. In today's gold value, it would be worth over 60 million," Don said, looking at Tanner before he started to relive loading the gold and his time in Alaska.

"You heard the general. Let's move it," he ordered his men. Don remembered seeing the US military plane take off.

He wished he was in Alaska looking for the gold and wished he knew what had happened to it.

Chapter 3

The Plot Thickens

It was a beautiful morning on Nov. 25th, 1941. Thunderclouds were backlit by the sun. The sound of an engine roared as the plane flew through the clouds flawlessly.

The U.S military cargo plane shared the same color as the gray clouds and camouflaged itself in the sky, but would that be enough to keep the crew and cargo safe?

Sergeant Bravo walked down the fuselage and made sure the men had their belts on and cigarettes out.

He reached Jones's seat.

"You need to put your seatbelt on, Mr. Jones."

"Why? When the plane goes down, I don't want to live," Jones mumbled under his breath so low that Sargent Bravo didn't hear.

Clover, the killer, sat next to him.

Garret and his co-pilot were busy making sure that the plane ran smoothly. Clover got up from his chair and went and stood between the pilot and the co-pilot, anchoring himself to the door that housed the cockpit.

Garret stared through the windshield and saw nothing but clouds.

"Those Japs are in for a whopping they won't soon forget," he said.

"They won't even know what hit them. Better put your seatbelt on. This could get a little rough," said the co-pilot to Clover.

Clover jumped onto the seat right behind the co-pilot but didn't put on his seatbelt. The plane began feeling turbulence as it moved through the clouds.

"Oh damn, getting kind of rough," said Clover. However, his comment was ignored as the pilot and co-pilot didn't respond and focused on their job.

"These clouds look amazing, don't they? It looks like God is about to cry," he said louder this time.

Garret turned and looked at him with a serious expression on his face.

"If these Japs aren't put down, we'll be crying too," he said as he stared back out at the clouds.

"You're right, I'm afraid," said Clover as he stood up from his seat, reached into the back of his waistband, and pulled out his handgun.

Garret plotted his path with caution; he set what was the best route to Russia and then turned back to look at Clover.

As he turned, he stared straight into the barrel end of Clover's gun pointed at his forehead. There was no time to scream or think before Clover pulled the trigger.

BANG!

Blood sprayed across the windshield as Clover turned around, aiming his gun at his new target, and pulled the trigger again.

BANG!

The next bullet went straight between the co-pilot's eyes, leaving a hole in his head. The co-pilot's body trembled, heaving once, and then went limp.

Now toward the end of the fuselage, Sargent Bravo turned and looked at the cockpit door when he heard the gunfire. Then Clover turned and put three bullets in him, and he fell to the floor.

Clover pulled Garret out of the seat as the plane lost altitude. Then, he pulled the control wheel back.

The plane took a sharp descent, then pulled back to level.

***

Meanwhile, four military men held onto their seats at the

back of the plane when the plane suddenly descended. As soon as it stabilized, they undid their seatbelts and got up.

In on the job, Junior pulled his gun and ordered the other three men to stand down.

The plane experienced continued light turbulence.

Junior, pointing his gun at the three other soldiers, said, "Stay over there, guys, and no funny business, this plane is being commandeered."

"I hope I don't have to use this," Junior said with sternness in his command.

Sergeant Jones, the mastermind behind the plot, was flung out of his seat during the descent. Finally getting himself together, he walked a little closer to the other men.

"I'd listen to him! We can do this one of two ways, either you do as you're told, or we kill you right now. It's that easy?" he said with a calmness in his voice.

"Raise your hand if you want to live, and you're going to do what you're told."

The three soldiers were quick to put their hands in the air.

Junior said, "There is plenty of work to be done once we land this plane."

Little did they realize that the plane did not completely regain its altitude to clear the mountaintop. The next instant, the plane hit the mountain slope ferociously, mowed down a dozen trees, lost its wings, and headed straight for an abandoned mine shaft.

Just as luck would have it, fate stepped in, and the plane hit the mine shaft head-on, killing everyone on board and packing itself in the mine shaft like a pea in a pod. Never to be seen again.

The snow dumped another five feet on the already three feet, covering the mine entrance and leaving no trace of the cargo plane or the gold.

***

A few years after, newspapers all across the country reported the surrender of Japan. But there was a backstory that had happened and was top-secret. It was not reported except in an obscure publication read by a few.

"As the United States dropped its atomic bombs on Hiroshima and Nagasaki in August 1945, 1.6 million Soviet troops launched a surprise attack on the Japanese army occupying eastern Asia. Within days, Emperor Hirohito's million-man army in the region had collapsed."

Slobodan Lekic, The Associated Press

The war was over.

Chapter 4

Forging Their Future

Tanner and Don stood in the driveway next to the Blazer that was to take Tanner and his friends to Alaska.

Tanner stood there and listened to his father talk, with a big suitcase and a backpack in the driveway.

"The person who finds that gold will become a national hero, worldwide celebrity, and very rich."

"Ahh yeah, I think you mentioned that at dinner; I'll keep that in mind when I'm reeling in that 50-pound salmon," Tanner said sarcastically. He finished his statement with, "I love you, dad."

"I know you have a little money saved, son, but I also know you don't have a job. So, ease my mind, let me give you a small stipend until your twentieth birthday. I'll give you $1,000 a month to help you get going in life, and if you need more to start a business, just ask."

Tanner didn't think he would need it but said, "Sure. If it makes you feel better, I'll take it."

"I didn't want to say it officially, but I probably won't be coming back. I'll take the stipend because I know it will make you and mom feel better. I don't want you guys to worry."

Tanner knew it was hard for his parents to let him go; they wanted him to do other things. But they put their desires aside and respected Tanner's decisions, as parents should.

"You know your mother and I have been planning your college ever since you were in Jr. High. Promise me that you will finish your photography training. Please finish what you started."

"You have my word," Tanner promised.

Tanner turned and put his backpack in the Blazer. Just then, Ken and Jon arrived with their gear, and they loaded it into the back of the Blazer.

Ken and Jon hugged Don and Wanda. They said their goodbyes and well wishes.

"Maybe I will see you at the end of the summer," Wanda said as she waved goodbye.

Tanner turned to look at his father and mother as his friends got in the car one last time.

He started the engine, backed out of the driveway, and headed in Canada's direction.

The three young men wanted to go to Alaska, all for

different reasons, but they all had something they were looking for. One thing was for certain. They would be setting their life journey in motion. The only thing similar in their journey was getting to Alaska.

***

The next morning, in Washington state now, the Pacific Ocean in view – on their way to Alaska. The brisk morning air was thick, the Seattle skyline and buildings in view out their side car window. The three young men were barreling down the highway.

“Let me see that picture of Angie again,” Ken asked Tanner, knowing damn well what she looked like.

Tanner multitasked driving, took out his wallet, pulled out a picture of Angie, and handed it over to Ken. “Boy, she's beautiful. I’ve always thought she was the prettiest girl in school.”

“Yeah! But she's not the only reason I need to go to Alaska. I guess you could say I'm chasing after a dream,”

Ken looked at him and handed the picture back.

“A big dream, I’m guessing,” he said with a smile.

“Yeah, I'm chasing after a dream too. I want to party till I die.”

Ken turned and looked at Jon, remembering that he was there too. He expressed his dream sarcastically.

"I guess we all have dreams," Ken mumbled.

"Nope, not all of us," Tanner said to them.

The guys took turns driving in 6-hour shifts. Then, after several stops for food, sleep, and bathroom breaks, in about 20 hours, Tanner and his friends arrived at the Canadian border.

As they approached the border crossing, the border town was in full swing.

In the driver's seat, Tanner said with disdain, "See, all these people, this is the type of thing I want to get away from."

"After we get through this crossing, let's stop at a liquor store and pick up a couple of six-packs of Labatt's Blue. I've heard it's a really tasty beer that you can only buy in Canada," Jon said as he tried to lighten the mood.

"Yeah, sounds like a good idea," Ken responded.

The car slowly moved in silence as the boys got lost in thought. After a good 20 minutes, they finally reached the border crossing.

Upon pulling up to the border gate, "Please step out of the vehicle, stand right here and show us some ID," said one border guard to Tanner.

The boys got out of the Blazer, and Tanner handed his ID to another border guard that walked up to him. As the border guard looked through Tanner's ID, he asked him, "Where are you young men going?"

Tanner spoke to the border guard that stood in front of him. "Going to Alaska for the summer, sir. If I like it, I might stay, but they'll be coming back after the summer."

The border guard asked another question as the other guard walked away with their documents.

"How much money do you young men have?" the main border guard asked as he handed back the ID cards.

"About $200 in cash and $3000.00 in traveler's checks between us," Tanner said.

"Any guns or fruit?" he asked.

"No, sir," Tanner said, ID card in hand.

"Can we see the paperwork for the dog?" asked the main border guard. The other guard said, "What is the dog's name?"

"That's King," Ken said.

Tanner pulled out papers from the car and handed them over. The first border guard glanced over them and handed them back over.

"You're good to go, boys. Enjoy your summer," the guard said as he handed back the papers, smiled, and walked away.

Tanner said out loud, “Northward,” as he pointed northward in a *Captain's Pose*.

He and his buddies got back in the car and crossed into Canada, heading for the ferry at the port at Prince Rupert. They drove through the Canadian backcountry, windows down, their shoulder-length hair blowing in the wind, music blaring. Ready to take on wild Alaska and everything it had to offer.

***

Ken was looking out the window, wowing over the scenic marvels they were witnessing.

“This wilderness is incredible. Look, there’s a moose.”

“Where?” Jon asked.

“Over there,” Ken pointed to a thicket of short trees in the tundra.

Grooving to the sound of music, Ken swung his hair back with his hand and looked behind. With furrowed brows, he wondered what Jon was doing in the backseat.

From a bag Jon kept near his leg, he fished out an unopened film container. Dubiously, Ken asked, “What’s that?”

Jon smirked as he glanced up and answered, “A little something for the road.”

While at home, before leaving for Alaska, Jon had taken out the film from the canister, stuffed it full of Thai Stick, and stuck it back in the box. Then he carefully resealed the box and put it in his camera bag.

As the stench of herbs diffused into the air, Tanner turned his head and grimaced at Jon.

"I can't believe you did that. I can't believe you jeopardized our whole future for a few joints! Why would you do something like that?"

Jon kept smiling and said, "Take it easy, man. The less that you knew about it, the better. Do you really think I would have brought it if you guys knew about it?

That's why I didn't say anything before. So, just chill. It won't be a problem. Don't worry. Just keep driving."

They drove 500 miles up the highway, pulling Tanner's dovetail trailer to Prince George, where they would be spending their first night in Canada.

Tanner noticed that the highway was being widened, and they were preparing the dirt road for pavement.

"Check out these D9 Cats," he said.

There was a lot of other road-building equipment on the side of the road too. When they drove just past Prince George, Ken said, “That looks like it might be a good turnout.”

They followed the dirt road back about a quarter mile and spotted a little turnout, where they parked the car, built a fire pit, and gathered wood for the night.

The mountains began to blur in the vastness of the red sky and the openness all around them.

“I could sure use a beer and a little smoke,” Jon said.

“Go ahead; I’m just enjoying the crackling of the fire and the night sky, my friend,” Tanner spoke as he climbed into his sleeping bag.

The next morning, they broke down the camp and drove the remaining 500 miles to the ferry at Prince Rupert.

They were yet to arrive in Alaska, yet the journey so far proved worthy of the adventure that lay ahead.

***

Chapter 5

The Day Has Come - The Ride up Alaska's Inside Passage

Tanner, Ken, and Jon were now waiting in line at the dock. A ferry ride was waiting for them. At the Prince Rupert ferry terminal, they marveled at the stillness of the sea and the greens merging with the blue at the ferry terminal dock.

The cascading nature of naturally carved mountains, high rising trees, and piercing blue skies. With so much color coming from one end of the sea to the base of the mountains, the water almost appeared green rather than blue.

It was truly a wonderful day, with the wind slightly blowing, the sun sharing its warmth, and the majestic mountains in the background. But this was only the start of *their* journey. Their eagerness to set foot in Alaska grew as they traveled each mile.

Especially Tanner's. He couldn't wait to have Angie back into his embrace, hold her and never let go. He wasn't ready to give up his thirst for a future with Angie.

***

After a few hours, the boys boarded the ferry and walked to the back deck. They stood next to the railing, the sea breeze gently blowing against their faces and music playing in the background.

It was like a scene from a movie. The ferry was moving steadily through the waters of the Inside Passage.

"Look at the size of those trees," Ken said, with thick treed, snowcapped mountains coming out of the seas and moving ever so slowly past them. The land was beaming with wildlife all around.

Tanner's camera was set on a tripod. He took a deep breath of fresh air into his lungs. Then, waiting for the right moment, he snapped a shot as an eagle flew by, with snowcapped mountains in the background.

"That's going to look nice hanging on someone's wall," he told Jon.

Jon had set up a tent on the back of the ferry so that they could sleep under the stars that night. But right now, he was lounging in a deck chair, taking in some sun rays, with his sunglasses on, with not a care in the world.

As Tanner was snapping pictures, a whale jumped a few hundred feet from the ship's port side.

Everyone by the rail marveled in awe as they witnessed the humpback whale perform a somersault as it shot out of the water.

Tanner wasn't ready for that one.

"Shoot, I missed that." It happened so fast, he mused.

As they approached Ketchikan, the dock was pretty full of people waiting for loved ones.

"We're going to have a few hours before the ferry will be leaving for the next stop," Ken said to the guys earlier.

Going to check out the town was next on the agenda. As they left the dock and walked onto the street, they saw a big welcoming signpost over the middle of the street that read, *"KETCHIKAN"* in big, red letters.

"Welcome To Alaska's First City, The Salmon Capital Of The World."

They spent their time at various tourist shops where they saw some incredibly intricate and beautiful ivory carvings and a lot of Tlingit Indian artifacts and attire.

"We have 30 minutes before we need to be back on that Ferry," Ken reminded the guys. They made it back with a lot of time to spare.

"Great. I think I will take up where I left off," Jon said as he pulled his sunglasses out of his backpack.

The hours ticked on, and the snow-covered peaks were now gleaming off in the distance, and the sea birds began to soar, indicating they were getting near the next port.

They stopped at Wrangell and Sitka but only briefly, on their way to Juneau and then to Skagway, where Angie was and had been all winter.

***

The full moon gleamed in the backdrop of snowcapped mountains. Tanner and Ken were leaning on the rail of the back deck of the ferry. Ken was deep in thought. Perhaps this was the best time to bring the topic up.

Ken asked Tanner, “Why don't you tell me about your dreams?”

Tanner was suspicious at first. Ken pushed for answers. Finally, Tanner conceded, “You sure you won't make fun like everyone else?”

Ken inclined his head sideways and replied, “Try me! I have dreams of my own. And some really lofty ones that I think I can make them happen in Alaska. So go on, tell me yours.”

Tanner started to tell him all about his dreams, “Well, it goes something like this, and this is the abbreviated version - I want to marry Angie. Then, settle down in a little cabin way out in Alaska somewhere, do some wildlife photography as a career, and…uh.” he stopped and looked at Ken for a second and then continued. "And do a little gold prospecting along the way."

The beats of the tunes, echoing through the ferry, were now a distant noise as the two had turned their attention away from it.

Tanner continued, "I just want to live my life happily and free. No drama. Just being a good man and having fun and adventure."

He shrugged and turned to look at the moon in the blue sky, unhindered by polluted air.

Ken patted his back and said, "Well, it looks like you are making good progress. You're heading in the right direction."

Tanner nodded.

"Yeah, but I have so far to go. And Jon almost ruined it for me."

"I'm sure he didn't mean anything by it," Ken reassured him.

"Yeah, but it's just the idea. You don't play around with someone else's future like that. That's my greatest fear. That I'm going to end up dead or in prison because of someone else's stupid doings," Tanner said.

Tanner took numerous shots as they approached Juneau the next day. The whales were mastering backflips and giving the sea birds a close shot. When the ferry stopped by the port in Juneau on the way to Skagway for a couple of hours, he caught a couple of dozen shots of the three of them in the festive downtown area as a parade played out and several others as they pulled away from the port.

***

Later that evening, on arriving in Skagway, in jubilation, Tanner pointed, "I think I see Angie!"

The other two looked around, unable to find any sign of her.

"Are you dreaming?" Ken asked. "Because I don't see her anywhere."

"Yeah, you'll need binoculars to see her from here," Jon joked.

Tanner pointed to her in the crowd again.

"There she is, with that girl, in purple! Do you see her now?"

He couldn't stop smiling. It had been so long since he had last seen her. Weeks and months had gone by. He was still holding on to the memories they had made last summer.

As they pulled into port, Tanner and Angie ran toward each other. Months of yearning and longing for each other, and now, they could finally be together. It was a long, warm embrace followed by a passionate kiss.

Still holding her close, Tanner took her hand, caressed it, and whispered, “My love, I've thought of you every day since I left on that ferry last year.”

He then pulled her back into another long hug as the stars twinkled above.

Chapter 6

Angie

Since last summer, Angie had been living in Skagway, living one of her dreams, dancing. Working at Soapy Smiths' old town saloon, dancing her way across the floors. Skagway was a busy tourist spot.

In recent years, Soapy Smith and his gang of thieves' stories were all the talk on the ferry ride up the inside passage.

Soapy Smith ran the town of Skagway with the gun when the gold rush was at its peak in the late 1890s.

In the midst of the tourist season, she made quite a name for herself as a dancer.

Every day she spent away from Tanner, she thought about her commitment to him. They had been away from each other for so long.

Angie was in her town hall dancing outfit when the two started to walk toward Tanner's Blazer. Jon and Ken were some steps ahead of them, having their own little talk.

"A lot has changed since you've been gone. I met

someone," Angie said, feeling slightly nervy.

At first, Tanner felt twitchy, but the next second, he regained his calm, held her hand, and said, "Honey, you know what, none of that matters to me."

He smiled at her and continued, "You are my soul mate, and I'm not willing to give up my dream with you without a huge fight."

Angie looked down and replied, "This could be… serious, you know?"

Tanner stopped as soon as he heard that statement.

'*What did she mean by that?'* he thought.

He clenched his teeth to process the thought that had slowly started to reside in his mind.

'Had she ACTUALLY fallen in love with her new man?'

Unfiltered, he said the next thought that came to his head out loud, "Have you had sex with him?"

Angie was dumbfounded. Instantly, she hit back, "Oh god, no! I don't even think about that at this point in my life. I thought … I thought you knew me better than that?"

Pulling her hand away from Tanner, she replied, her voice crisp, "I have college and a career to think about. Why would you..."

She turned into a red gumball as the anger overpowered her.

"My parents may have led me to believe that sex is the *"be all, end all"* to human existence, but I have my own dreams to follow and a vision for my future. A prosperous one, for Lord's sake, Tanner. What made you think I'd do that? I do have common sense you know?" she stated.

Her eyes glowed with molten lava, reflecting anger building up inside her.

She took a deep breath in order to calm herself down. But the question he asked struck at her instantly and was appalling. She was definitely not anticipating that.

Angie took Tanner's hand. She traced his eyebrows with her fingers to ease his fears and replied, "Tanner, you know, I want to be with *you*. You know how much I love you, don't you? When I talk of my dreams, *you are* always part of my visions and dreams."

The reassurance brought a smile to Tanner's face, and he caressed her cheeks with his palm while replying, "I am so glad to hear those words coming from you, honey. Because you know we can make this whole thing go away."

With a puzzled look on her face, she asked, "How?"

Tanner's smile widened, and he replied, "You just watch."

"I'm trying out this old theory. Watch the Universe bend to the heart of man," he continued, looking into Angie's eyes.

She returned the passion that was building up in his eyes, reflecting it, and concurred, "I believe in that theory too."

Tanner kissed her on the forehead and said, "That is what I love about you. Your common sense, your beauty, and a heart that seeks for what's right, always."

Angie added, "You know doing right means everything to me, but sometimes life can be confusing. I think… religion is the main reason for all the killings and chaos in the world."

Nodding, Tanner replied, "You are right. But you're talking about *man's religion. Not* the religion of *love*. You would have to be blind to not see the beauty and love all around us. In humanity, in the human body, in nature, the stars and the Earth."

He held her hand, and the two started to walk along the street again.

"Everything man has put his hand to, he has ruined or brought chaos to. But we are a relativity young world and a very young nation," Tanner continued, "and one day, we will get it right."

Since he knew that the topic was now closing in on a volatile point dangerously, he skillfully changed the subject of their conversation.

“I wonder what the old cabin looks like?” he asked her.

Curious, Jon heard him say this and abruptly stopped in his way, turned to look behind, and asked, “What old cabin?”

“I told you guys about the old cabin that Angie and I camped at when we were here last summer,” Tanner replied.

“It’s in the Dyea Valley,” Angie added.

They were now closing in on Tanner’s Blazer that was outside Soapy Smith’s Saloon. In their tie-dyed printed shirts, trekking boots, khaki, and green hiking shorts, everyone around them could tell that these young people were full of thrill and adventure. In their early twenties, as was apparent from their demeanor and long hair, it wasn’t hard to make out how carefree they were.

Their exuberant attitude, mannerisms, and how they carried themselves clearly indicated their adventurous lifestyle.

“Why don't we take a ride out there?” suggested Ken.

Angie and Tanner looked at each other and then at Jon and Ken and nodded, agreeing to take a ride.

The four of them, along with King, barreled down an old dusty road on their way to the old cabin.

When they finally got there and got out of the Blazer, Tanner was surprised.

“This doesn't look anything like it did when I left last summer…” he said.

“It flooded last year. Old-timers around here say that it was the seventh time the river came over its banks since gold miners built it almost 100 years ago, eager to cross over into Alaska and Canada's Interior,” Angie said.

Tanner looked at Ken and said, “In December, most of the eagles in Alaska and the Yukon come to this river valley to feast and feed on the hooligan fish. This is the only ice-free water outlet in Alaska in the winter.”

The old cabin was 16'x16'x6' with a sod roof, decaying shudders on the windows, and about two inches of mud and dirt blanketed the floor. With an eye for beauty through the eye of a camera, Tanner crouched down and clicked off more photos of the picturesque sight.

Although it was muddy, it looked aesthetically pleasing from the camera’s lens, told a great story, and took some awesome photos.

Ken looked around and pointed out, “This is really nice, but we need to start thinking about work. I only have enough money to last about two or three months. And if we keep spending at this rate, we are going…I can’t…”

Tanner nodded, "Maybe I can sell some of my photos. But really, we don't need to worry about money too much. My dad is rich. We can fall back on him for like six months or so if we have to.

Besides, our major expenses have already been paid."

"That reminds me, I need to go buy my plane ticket. Angie, is there a travel agent in town? I'm planning on going home at the end of summer," Jon said.

Tanner, Ken, and Angie turned toward him, squinting their eyebrows, astonished.

"We just got here. Think about that some other time."

"You know there isn't an airport here," Angie said.

"Yeah, I figured that," Jon said, looking around.

"You'll have to take the ferry back down to Juneau or drive up to Anchorage to fly out."

"At the end of summer, we will probably be closer to Anchorage," Tanner added as he snapped his head and finger-combed his shoulder-length hair back, falling to his face.

"You should probably plan on flying out of there," he continued.

With Byrd's turn, turn, turn, playing in the car, Jon smirked and replied, "Who knows, maybe I will like it here and stick around. Or I've always wanted to go to Kathmandu, in Nepal. Yeah, maybe I'll go there. I have nothing holding me down anymore."

Ken patted his back and said, "Now, I would really think about that one. They say there are rats the size of cats there."

All of them laughed while Jon added, "Yeah, and they say the *hash* there is the best in the world.

"Is that all you think about? You need to start making plans for your future, Jon. You know you're going to get out of life what you're willing to put into it," Tanner said.

Jon shrugged and replied, "I told you I do have plans for my future. I'm going to party till I die. That's my plan, and I'm sticking to it."

***

Under the endless blanket of sky, the stars twinkling overhead and the moonlight showing bright, they boarded the state ferry and traveled the short distance to the other side of the bay.

Soon, the four of them sat around the campfire they threw together for the evening, with hundreds of eagles in the trees on the bank of the river valley.

Chapter 7

Mountain Man Extraordinaire

In the mid-summer morning a few days later, when the sun rose on the horizon, and the snow-capped mountains glistened in the distance, north of the city of Haines, Alaska. Tanner, Angie, Ken, and Jon, along with King, looked forward to traversing through the area that boasts the Chilkat Bald Eagle Preserve, the Glacier Bay National Park, and the mountain trails that hit the list of most hikers. But before they could go ahead with their hike, they wanted to know the best place to go in the area.

As the four got out of Tanner's Blazer, they saw a middle-aged man coming in their direction. They guessed he was in his early thirties from the way he looked. Wearing a red and green plaid shirt, with khaki pants and heavy boots, flaunting an overgrown stubble and curly shoulder-length dark brown hair, he walked confidently and smiled when he noticed Tanner looking at him.

The mountain man, his persona as colorful as his dressing style, walked out of the café beside the gas station.

Tanner returned the smile and walked up to him, striking up a conversation.

“Excuse me? My name is Tanner,” he said and stretched out his hand.

“Hi, I’m Michael,” and the two shook hands.

“Do you know of any good places in the area to hike? Me and my friends, Angie, Ken, and Jon.” Tanner pointed to his crew. “We are here visiting the area and are looking for a good place to hike. Can you suggest any place?”

Michael smiled. “Boy, Howdy! You’ve come to the right place. I’ve come here five summers in a row, and if you go down that road, half a mile, you’ll come to a state park.”

He pointed to his left and then continued, “Hike the trail to the top, and you’ll end up on a plateau. This is the perfect time of the day and season to do it. The wildflowers are in full bloom, and you’ll have a three-hundred and sixty-degree view of the snow-capped mountain range. It’s awesome up there!”

This lit up Tanner, Angie, Jon, and Ken’s moods, and Tanner asked, “How long is the hike?”

“It’s about an hour and a half through a *magical forest*,” Michael replied.

“Wait. Before we go, do they have any good food in this town?” Jon asked.

Ken stepped in. “Because…” instead of completing the

sentence, he pointed toward his growling, half-starved tummy and smiled.

Michael shrugged and said, “I mean, the food is *okay* if you like putting garbage in your machine.”

Angie pulled Ken back when she saw and heard Michael's reaction and added, “Let me ask the question in a better way.”

She winked and then turned to Michael, “Are there any good restaurants or health food stores around?

Upon hearing this, Michael nodded and answered, “Yeah! There’s a health food store and restaurant about two blocks down that dirt road.”

He smiled and then added, “But I’ve got a better idea.”

Tanner and Ken looked at him with anticipation and raised eyebrows, “We're listening.”

“Why don’t you grab a few things from the store and come to my place, and we can put together a lunch? And then I’ll go with you on the hike and be your guide?” suggested Michael.

The four friends were all smiles upon hearing this. “Sounds good. I like it!” Tanner said.

Angie smiled, “I’m up to it. Let’s do it.”

Standing next to Michael, Tanner asked, “Are there any

good places to take pictures? That's what I do. Love to capture moments on the camera."

"As a matter of fact, this is the perfect place. Stand right there. Angie, Ken, Jon, get King in the picture too," Tanner proceeded.

"You will be amazed, mate," Michael replied, standing in the pose with his new friends.

***

Soon after, all five strolled from one shelf to another at the health food store. Collecting items for lunch and the next few days, walking alongside Tanner, Angie whispered, "I have a good feeling about this."

Tanner smiled and said, "So do I, sweetness."

After visiting the health food store, they followed Michael to his place, a few miles from town. They pulled up to a yurt with a twelve-by-twelve entry to the dwelling, set a hundred feet back on the side of the dirt road.

Pulling into the driveway, clearly enthralled by how nice the yard looked and how well the yurt had been constructed, Tanner declared, "Now this is what I call a house!"

A yurt is a Mongolian tent built out of 2x2s, circular in shape.

Raising an eyebrow, Angie responded, “You would *never* get me to live in something *that* small. I need a washer, dryer, and a nice stove to bake with.”

“Let’s see what he has before you say anything.”

As they walked back to the driveway covered in dusty summer dirt, they were taken back by what they saw. The realization struck them that they were in for a once-in-a-lifetime chance meeting and hiking experience.

This was no *ordinary* man. He seemed more like an Alaskan mountain *man extraordinaire*, all set for the Alaskan experience.

They walked onto the steps of entry of his yurt, which was clearly customized and hand-built.

Upon entering, they walked into the kitchen area made out of exotic woods and built with professional craftsmanship. Woodworking that you would only find in an expensive trimaran or yacht.

In amazement at the craftsmanship, they were in awe of the structure's beauty.

They walked through the 12 x12 entry, which was the kitchen, where the beauty shined.

A square 8’ walled structure in the middle of the yurt

housed a bathroom. On the adjoined wall outside the bathroom, a laundry area was adjacent to which a few trophy fish and game heads were hanging.

In the middle of the yurt, at the high point of the tent, a beautiful circular 5' stained glass window depicted a fishing and hunting scene.

As they walked along the inside perimeter of the yurt, they saw some pictures hanging on the wall and walked over.

Gazing at them in admiration, Tanner asked, "Did you bag all these yourself?"

Michael answered, "Every head you see in these pictures I took with a bow."

"Where is the sport in using a rifle?" he said. "I like to give the poor animal a chance to live. And everything I take, I eat."

There were many stuffed fish on the walls and many nicely framed photos of Michael in the backcountry, posing with his prizes alongside a floatplane on a beautiful river or a lake with mountains in the background.

Inspired by Michael's adventures and achievements, Ken said, "Looks like you're living the dream!"

"Got to. You only have one go-round at this life. So, you might as well live it to the fullest," responded Michael.

"That is my dream, right there!"

Ken pointed to a floatplane pulling up to a dock with cargo and moose pelt waiting to be picked up.

"I dream of being an Alaskan bush pilot!"

Michael said, "Well, it will happen if you put your mind to it. The mind and the will can make incredible things happen. I have used positive projection many times."

"But the first thing is, you have to have a vision. You have to know where you want to go in life."

Tanner, Angie, Ken, Jon, and their new tour guide, Michael, were getting ready for the hike, putting on their hiking boots, and packing their hiking gear into well-used packs. King, the big handsome malamute that had been giving Tanner and his crew good company throughout their trip, was waiting outside the yurt, all geared up for the trek.

While Michael was putting in a few last items in his pack and zipping it up, Tanner commented, "Those are some nice pants."

"Thanks, buddy," Michael said.

"So, what is it that you do?" he asked.

"Funny you ask. I'm a fashion designer in Chicago. More specifically, I design men's sportswear."

Tanner was clearly astonished by this revelation.

"You mean like those pants?" he questioned.

Michael had rugged, durable Gortex twenty-first-century hiking pants on that Tanner had never seen before. They looked like Carhart's with hammer loops, reinforced pockets, and knee patches. The pants were colored like burnt orange with foot-long black reinforcement patches over the knee area.

Michael nodded, "Exactly! You won't see pants like these on the market for twenty years or more."

He pulled the pant out and held the material between his thumb and index finger, feeling its touch.

"See this fabric. It's called Gortex. It is still in its developmental stage as of now. This fabric has not even been introduced to the public yet."

"How did you get a hold of it?" Tanner asked while feeling the fabric himself.

Letting go of his pant, he threw his backpack over his shoulder and replied, "I work with the company patenting it."

Tanner was surprised that his new friend, who resembled more of a hippie, did so much.

***

They were now heading for the forest, around some boulders covered in green, living moss with stalactite gleaming in the sun.

"I've never seen boulders like these before."

"Well then, just wait till you see the trees."

Just then, Angie called out loud, "Tanner! You've got to see this."

Tanner looked around in her direction and responded, "Coming, love, what is it?"

When he stood beside her, he noticed what had gripped her. The tree limbs were loaded with vibrant green moss, and the leaves were a vibrant blue/green. The root system that blanketed the forest floor looked like a tapestry of interwoven blood vessels.

The hiking trail was right alongside a three-foot-wide creek winding down the mountain. Boulders and living green moss littered the trees, with stalactite shimmering everywhere.

As the five of them went along the trail, hiking through the forest, they stopped near a tree they found along the trail, with the creek running through it. It truly was a magical hike.

Standing tall and high above Haines, his hair flowed with the wind. Tanner clicked dozens of pictures and continued his hike upward. Upon reaching the mountain top, he set up his tripod stand

and the camera on the highest point and started to capture the beauty of the snowcapped mountain range in his clicks to keep as a souvenir of this journey.

"My mother was right!" Ken exclaimed with Angie by his side. Then, he yelled, "This is God's country!"

The echo of his voice ricocheted back from the lofty peaks they were surrounded by and brought a smile to both Angie and Ken's faces, only adding to their excitement.

Tanner panned the camera three hundred and sixty degrees, recording the beauty of the snow-capped mountains.

***

Back at the Chilkat State Park parking lot, ready to drive back when Angie said, "You were right, Michael, *that* was *amazing*."

"I concur! That was one heck of a hike," Tanner added.

"Where to now?" Angie asked.

Michael responded, "Why don't we go back to my place, throw together a few sandwiches, and you guys can be on your way."

"Sounds like a plan to me!" Tanner said.

Chapter 8

Southcentral Alaska

Weeks went by, and they had stopped in Valdez, Alaska, before heading to Los Anchorage, the big city of the north.

It was a sight to see and a marvel! The pipeline was on the verge of being finished, and they got to witness the pipe being laid.

A group of men slopped around a wet and muddy section of pipe that was being fitted and welded.

Nearby was a pile of sacked pipe, 6 to a stack; 3 on the bottom, 2 in the middle, and 1 on top - every 65 feet, for as far as the eye could see. The pipes themselves were 36" in circumference and about 50' long.

Heavy equipment was moving around. The men were preparing the mountainside for its next link of pipe to be fitted on its long journey to the holding station at Valdez.

The friends saw a small caterpillar anchored to a larger one. The smaller caterpillar winch cable was hooked on to the larger one parked at the top of the grade. The smaller one was smoothing the grade on a very steep valley that the pipe was to travel through.

Meanwhile, another group of men were attaching a cable and shackle to a fifty-foot piece of pipe that they were lifting with a crane. This was to be the next link in the pipeline project, and the welders were all working to lay its base.

***

One morning when the sun was out and its warmth coalesced with the cool morning breeze, the four friends stopped by a coffee shop to awaken their drowsy souls. The table across the far end, at the right corner, was empty, so they decided to settle there.

Tanner and his crew discussed their next action plans while sipping their coffees and having French toast and scrambled eggs.

That's when Tanner heard a couple of old-timers on the booth right behind theirs talk about a familiar legend, *The Legend of Lost Wartime Gold.*

Tanner indicated his friends to zip their lips, gesturing with his fingers, and listened carefully to the conversation behind them.

One of the old men said in his croaky voice, "I don't know how accurate this is, but I was reading this article about a secret war-time transfer of gold right before the attack on Pearl Harbor. The US was paying Russia to help us fight Japan just before the Japs surprise military strike. It said we were sending over cigarettes and blankets *with the gold*."

"The legend says it had almost 6 million worth of gold bars and that the military plane carrying it hit bad weather around Mt. St. Ellis and went down with seven men on board. They were never to be heard of again."

The second man then asked, "Did they say what path the flight had taken?"

To this, the first man replied, "Well, according to the article, it was somewhere within fifty square miles on the south ridge. They also showed a map of the area that they thought it might be. But it is all speculation."

"Can you imagine what that gold would be worth today?" asked the second man.

"Probably fifty or sixty million or more," guessed the first.

Their eyes widened in astonishment when Tanner and his friend heard it. Tanner smiled, put the money for the bill on their table, and said in a hushed yet excited tone, "That's what my dad was talking about… But he said he helped load it."

The temperatures were now cooling down, turning a bit into sweater season, and the colors of leaves that amassed the plains and forests of Alaska were starting to transform from viridescent to a mix of rusty orange and yellow. They lined the streets, appeasing the pedestrians by the crunch of their crisped forms as they stepped on them.

Like most others, the onset of fall brought about a feeling of loss of freedom in the friends exploring the Alaskan spectacles.

They pulled up into the parking lot of the pipeline club in the makeshift pipeline worker city of Valdez in the semi-darkness of twilight. The trailer homes were everywhere around. The summer of 1976 had come to an end, and it was time for them to start thinking about work.

***

"Boy, I could really use a cold brew about now. How about we step into that bar up ahead and see if they will sell us a few beers," suggested Ken as they headed into the mud-drenched town of Valdez, the endpoint of the Trans-Alaska Pipeline.

Tanner acknowledged, "Sounds good to me. I hope they don't card us." As they pull up to the front of the mud hole of a building

While sitting in the blazer, Ken replied with a smirk on his face, "All they can do is throw us out."

Pushing the door to the entry of the pipeline club open, Tanner looked around and added, "Let's sit at a table by the door in case we need to make a quick exit."

Really, they were on the hunt for work. “Maybe we’ll get lucky and meet someone that knows of some work,” Tanner said to Ken.

The sky had a tinge of orange as the rays of the sun spread through the majestic mountains and reflected off the icy surfaces of the tidewater. The band at the pipeline club where Tanner and Ken were visiting was playing the bridge over troubled water in the background when the two ordered beers.

The young waitress, her wavy amber brown hair tied in a messy bun, placed their order on the table and asked, “Are you new in town?”

Tanner smiled and replied, “Yeah, we’re up from California looking for some work for the summer.”

The rectangular name badge that the waitress had on read *JJ*. Tanner noticed Ken outright staring at her and grinned. It was expected of him, Tanner thought, for the waitress was very pretty.

“Are you serious? I was just talking to a guy who is looking for a couple of guys to help at a cement plant.”

“Go talk to that guy over there, wearing the cream polo shirt. Tell him JJ sent you.”

While Tanner and Ken talked with JJ’s connection about getting a job, Tanner noted how Ken’s eyes were glued to the beautiful waitress. The attraction between them was obvious because JJ kept throwing glances his way every now and then, too.

Finally, Tanner nudged Ken. “Why don’t you go talk to her,” he encouraged him.

“I can handle this on my own.” Ken grinned.

If things went in the direction that fate was leading, it would end only one way.

In the darkness of the night, when the flying squirrels and bats came out of their digs, the trailer enunciated the aura of pleasure and excitement. Unsuppressed moans of Ken and JJ rang out in the compact space of her tiny trailer.

***

Back at the pipeline club the next evening, Tanner, Angie, Ken, Jon, JJ, and her girlfriend, Kristy, were sitting at a table. They noticed a woman in her early thirties, wearing a striped pink and white shirt and bell-bottom jeans. Her long black hair leisurely fell three-quarter way to the floor. She was moving from one table to another and looked right at home.

Nodding toward her, Tanner asked JJ, “What’s up with her?”

JJ smiled while answering, “*That* woman there? Well, you are looking at the richest woman in Valdez.”

"*And* the hardest working!" added Kristy.

JJ nodded, "They say she pulls in about 5 grand a week, pulling the train."

Tanner and the crew were not amazed.

"Do you know her personally?" asked Tanner.

JJ shook her head and replied, "No! She keeps to herself."

"They say she sends the money home to her parents," Kristy said.

Just then, the woman headed for the door, gave a whistle, and raised her hand with a pointing gesture. Soon, about 20 rugged-looking Alaskan pipeline workers, wearing dirty boots, worn-out jeans, and jackets, walked out of the club behind her.

They were all either flaunting overgrown beards or a walrus mustache and had dirty clothes and muddy shoes. And all had money burning a hole in their pockets.

***

Tanner, Angie, Jon, and Ken had rented an apartment near the cement company where Ken and Tanner had started to work at.

Early one morning, a few months into their stay in town, Tanner was standing on the balcony. He looked down at the street and reiterated that the town was too small for them.

While leaving for work, Tanner and Ken were walking out of the door, and the phone in the apartment started to ring.

On the other end, a 20-year-old scrappy local boy was on the receiver and picked a pointless fight.

"When you get to work, I'm going to kick your ass, California boy!"

"I'll tell you what," Ken replied. "If you can or can't kick my ass, I'll buy you a case of beer and fill up your gas tank."

When Ken showed up at the site, the bully had his shirt off, and Ken started to pull his sweater off. The local bully came right at him. Quickly, Ken pulled his sweater back down and proceeded to fight the bully.

The fight went on for what seemed like hours, but Ken finally got the upper hand, holding his shoulders down with his knees and walloping the bully's face until it was a bloody mess.

Eventually, the other workers at the job site pulled Ken off before he ended up doing more damage. The bully's eyes were so bruised and bloodied that beneath his eye sockets, his cheekbones were exposed. His face was unrecognizable when Ken got through with him.

After the fight, the bully's friends loaded him into his raised "75" Ford truck.

Ken walked to Tanner's Blazer. Tanner had given Ken a ride to work and witnessed the whole situation unfold.

Ken went for his wallet on the seat, walked over to the bullies' truck, and threw the bullies' friend a 50-dollar bill.

"That should cover a case of beer and a tank of gas," he said, as they looked at him like he was from another planet.

Ken then walked back to Tanner's Blazer to get some tools when Tanner asked, "How much did you give him?"

While pulling the tools out of the back of the blazer, Ken answered, "Fifty."

"FIFTY DOLLARS?" he exclaimed, "Hey, you want to fight after work? I could use a case and a tank full," Tanner said with a smile.

***

Tanner, Angie, Ken, and Jon were sitting around the apartment they had rented for their time in Valdez when the boredom got so thick that they could cut it with a knife.

"I feel that this town is getting too small for us," Tanner said.

Raising an eyebrow, Ken remarked arrogantly, "Yeah, I feel it's time to head for the big city of the North, Los Anchorage.

"I could use a change of scenery myself!" mused Angie.

Chapter 9

Tanner and Angie Get Married

Eighteen months after their venturesome stay in Alaska, Tanner and Angie went back to California for a brief visit and to make their love for each other public.

It was finally the day Tanner and Angie had waited so long for. Their love had survived months of separation, and here they were all set to walk hand in hand forever and take their marriage vows.

On a fine afternoon in the summer of 1978, out in the back yard of Tanner's father's house, Don McKenzie and a couple-hundred guests were mingling. The preacher was in the yard with an anxious and happy look on his face.

Tanner was dressed in a black tuxedo, a bow tie, and a well-tailored white dress shirt underneath. Don McKenzie said, adjusting his bow tie, "I'm so happy for you both, son. But what is the deal with Angie's parents?"

It was five minutes till count down. They had still not made it to the wedding.

Tanner shrugged and replied, “This is the type of thing she has dealt with all her life.”

Tanner looked toward the far corner of the yard where Angie was sitting with her friends, chatting about something he wasn’t aware of.

But the topic of their conversation wasn’t his concern. The moment he saw Angie walk into the yard, dressed in her white off-the-shoulder lace dress that pronounced her slender figure, made her look like a goddess.

He was dazzled by her grace and elegance as she smiled, maintaining her sophistication and grandeur.

‘Yeah, I could spend the rest of my life waking up to that beautiful face,’ raced across his mind.

Don glanced at his watch and said, “They are half an hour late!”

Tanner shook his head, adding, “This is nothing. They didn’t even bother to show up when she graduated from college.

They called her from Hawaii at the last minute and said they were stuck there because of a drug deal gone bad.”

Don was taken by surprise.

“They are good people. They just get into some bad situations,” Tanner answered.

Don said, “As I’ve always said, God gave us the ability to make choices, but the consequences are out of our hands.”

Tanner let out a sigh and stated, “I can't wait to hear their excuse this time.”

Just then, Angie’s parents crashed the party - drunk, loud, and boisterous.

“We left our camera at home,” Angie’s mother said. “So, we turned around to go home and get it.

“And we almost rolled the car,” Her dad added, “Lucky we were able to get back on the road and back home.”

“And now we’re back here... just a little late,” added her dad, raising his glass.

Her mom said, “We just had to have a drink when we got home. We were so shaken.”

Brushing her statement off, her dad said, “She was. Honestly, I enjoyed the ride.”

Tanner looked over to Angie and saw how embarrassed she looked upon her parent’s entry, so late and drunk.

Right then, Tanner and Angie’s eyes met, and Tanner smiled a little, assuring her that all was well. Sparkle-eyed, she returned the gesture wholeheartedly.

The preacher, who was, until then, standing in the corner, vexed because it was getting late, had now taken his place on the stage.

"Wait!" exclaimed Angie's dad, and everyone looked at him, confused. "Wait, let me get my camera out first."

Boiling with anger, the preacher rolled his eyes, and almost every guest in their seats either sighed in annoyance or groaned.

***

The sun cast its shadows, peeping between the trees when the maid of honor walked in, holding a flower bouquet. A 3-year-old flower girl dressed in her cute pink dress walked in front, throwing flowers as they walked down a long white carpet spread through a row of about 200 guests seated on Don and Wanda's backyard lawn.

The setup with the white Dahlias and the purple, pink and white Lisianthus sitting gracefully amid the greens gave the ceremony a fine look—an exquisite paid-for wedding retreat.

Geese were swimming, sun rays were flickering on the river that bordered the property, and the white pillars on both edges of the yard were draped with white fabrics and flowers springing from them. The covered swing benches were well utilized by the guests.

There was a dancing stage at the center, with a good-sized gable on the side, with the trees covering the yard's edges made the setup feel like a true wedding paradise.

The guests were in their seats when Angie came down the aisle holding her father's arm. Her father was taking a noticeable high step, like an ex-marine.

As Tanner and Angie took the stage, the preacher announced, "Dearly beloved, we are gathered here today to join Tanner McKenzie and Angie Wilson into an everlasting union."

After some blessed words, the preacher said, "What God has joined, let no man try to part, or they can expect an everlasting damnation setting over them… I now pronounce you man and wife.

Tanner and Angie, may you kiss forever," he said, and the two kissed with Jackson Brown's, somebody's baby playing in the background.

After the ceremony, everyone gathered near the stage, holding up their cameras and taking videos and photos of the special day.

The family stood beside the bride and groom, and the cameras clicked hundreds of times. They posed for pictures in the backdrop of a beautifully decorated pillared setting, the river flowing in the background, and geese taking a dip in the water.

Everyone settled as Ken was now at the wedding table, ready to give the toast.

He stood up and clicked his spoon on his wine glass, getting everyone's attention.

"Someone once told me the key to a successful marriage is falling in love with the same person every day," He stated while smiling at the newlywed couple.

He then raised his glass and said, "I would like to say that you two have set out on a journey of friendship, love, and marriage that will last a lifetime.

God has only begun to shape your lives into the one He has ordained and blessed because of your faithfulness to your dreams and each other."

Turning back to Tanner, he said, "Tanner, I see you as a pillar among men, a strong oak. And I have a gut feeling that God will show Himself and bless you in ways you can't imagine."

He then pointed toward Angie and said, "And Angie, you are the envy of every woman. Beautiful in every way and a woman after the heart of God with a soul and heart of pure gold.

What a team the two of you make. It's as if the eagle met the sky.

With that, I ask for blessings on this sacred day."

He walked over and kissed the bride and clutched the groom in good wishes, then still standing, with wine glass high in the air, he said, "Don, Wanda, I love you guys,"

He blew kisses in their direction.

"Grandma McKenzie, Linda, the whole family, I love you!"

Pointing toward the other attendees with his glass, "DJ's, caters, thanks for making this happen. And everyone that could make it, thanks a lot."

A moment later, Tanner and Angie were on the gable dance floor. It was covered with flowers blooming on the sides and its roof in a warm embrace. Just then, Tanner's grandma cut in, followed by Angie's father, and next came the crowd.

***

After the guests departed the party, Tanner, Angie, and Ken were in the McKinzie home.

"I wonder what Jon is doing these days. I sure wish he could have made it to the wedding," Angie said.

Tanner pulled back the strand of hair falling on her face and said, "Last I heard, he was heading for Nepal. Kathmandu, I believe, is what he said."

He continued, “Sounds like he's living his dream. It’s amazing how dreams become a reality.”

Angie said, caressing his back, “Why don't you call his mother and see if she has heard anything from him?”

“I know his mom pretty well. So, I'll give her a call in a while,” said Ken.

A short time later, Tanner and Angie stood by each other, observing Ken as he talked with Jon’s mother. Then, they saw the smile on his lips fade away.

“I'm so sorry for you and Jon. I can't imagine what you are going through. Life is so fragile. One day you can be sitting on top of the world, and the next… well, you know.”

Angie held Tanner’s hand, their fingers interlaced, and the two looked at each other in confusion, waiting for the news.

Ken said, “Okay, Miss Lay, I'll let Tanner and Angie know. And you can be sure that you guys are in our prayers. Take care. Bye.”

“What was that about?” Tanner asked when Ken hung up.

“You guys need to sit down for this,” he said as he approached the two of them.

“What?” Angie tightened her grip on Tanner.

Ken motioned and reiterated, “I'm serious, sit.”

Tanner and Angie sat, and Ken started to explain.

“Well, it seems like Jon got himself arrested in Kathmandu, and they’re going to execute him in three weeks.”

“What!?” Tanner jolted up. “Are you serious? I tried to warn him!”

“His mom said she has a lot of attorneys working to get him out, but it doesn't look good,” Ken said as he plopped himself down on the couch.

Chapter 10

Life Is What Happens When We Are Busy Making Plans

It was another awesome summer morning in Alaska after getting back from the wedding, with a bright sun shedding its light on the slow-dancing waves on the shore of Montana Creek, a well-known tributary of the Susitna River. At least fifty fishermen were fishing the bend in the Creek. The creek was about 25 feet wide, and the bend in the creek was a quarter mile long, situated right off the Parks HWY.

The bridge was heavily packed with parked cars, and the dirt side roads were filled with campers and cars. The nearby spots were crowded with people everywhere. Tanner and Ken were part of the people lining the riverbank.

"I'm going to catch the biggest fish you ever saw," Tanner said confidently.

"The fish I'm going to catch will make your fish look like a French fry," Ken claimed amusingly.

Right after he finished saying that, he felt a jerk on his

fishing rod. Sure enough, he had a monster on his line.

"FISH ON!" he exclaimed.

People on the shore saw that he had a fish on and started cheering him on as he fought against the big fish.

Then they began to reel their lines in to give him more room.

As he battled the fish, he waded high into the water.

"Yeah, ride that puppy!" Tanner cheered.

After a long fight with the monster, Ken finally managed to pull it onto the shore. The fish was huge.

"Looks like that thing might last us the winter," Tanner said enthusiastically.

"Angie is going to pop a cork when she sees this monster," Ken replied.

After a good day on the river, they walked back to the blazer with the ice chest full of fish. Ken had the monster by the gill and over his shoulder. It was so huge that the tail was almost dragging on the ground.

***

A few weeks passed, the sun was slipping away, and the moon was slowly making its way up the sky while Tanner, Angie, and Ken were hanging off a sheer rock cliff. It was nearly 1000 feet above the valley. Under the foggy sky, they felt flashes of cold, but the slow wind made them feel right at home.

"When will we get after that gold we've been talking about for years?" Ken questioned.

"I say we stop talking about it and get busy doing some research and planning," Tanner answered.

"We are all in the best climbing shape of our lives, at least I feel I am," Angie added.

"Wait a minute, love. You're the best thing about me. If I lost you, I would have no reason to live. You will oversee the ground operations, the most critical of all the things we will be doing," Tanner stated.

Hanging off the side of the cliff in sleeping bags that were tethered to the cliff on a cold morning, Ken takes a bite of his omelet and a swig of coffee.

"I'll be flying the plane, and this is what I've learned about the gold."

Ken recounted what they all knew. "In 1941, right before the attack on Pearl Harbor, a cargo plane carrying a shipment of about 6,000,000 worth of gold bars was bound for Russia. Medical supplies, cigarettes, and blankets were also onboard.

Russian officials were eager to help the US fight the Japanese. They were having their own issues with the country. The article mentioned that, '*The US Army struck a deal. But the plane never made it. Instead, it went down over the Wrangell-Saint Ellis mountains with the gold and five soldiers on board.*'"

"How many times have we gone over that?" Tanner threw into the conversation.

Angie quickly responded, "About a thousand."

Ken pulled a map out of his bag and said, "National Geographic says it went down right in this area."

Ken pointed out the location on the map to Tanner and Angie.

Tanner looked at Angie with a sparkle in his eye and said, "There have been several attempts at finding the plane, but no one has been successful until us."

He rubbed his hands.

Angie furrowed her brows in jest and smiled.

"Oh, quit it!" she said.

On the way back to the car the next morning, mosquitoes swamped them by the thousands. The attacking army of the mosquitoes were not the dime-sized ones that one could see and swat, but they were the really small ones. They were called No-see-ums for a good reason.

Angie yelled. "These mosquitos are horrible. I'm going to run for the car!"

"I'm right behind you, love!" Tanner exclaimed.

"Hold up, I'm coming too!" Ken starts to run.

Halfway back to the blazer, they stopped in their tracks. There was a baby moose on the trail. They suspected the mama was not far away. Then they heard the sound of the undergrowth and vegetation bending and snapping as a big, towering mama moose revealed herself; Tanner, Ken, and Angie stayed frozen, hoping the moose wouldn't see them as a threat.

However, she started wagging her tongue from side to side and digging in the dirt with her hoof; it was more than clear that she was getting ready to charge them.

Without giving it another thought, the three turned and started to run. They slowed down as they dodged through the bushes to escape the mama moose and safely got to their car.

***

It had been a few months into the summer since they discussed the gold at the sheer cliff. Angie was now on the job at a gold dig for her summer employer. They were working at a mining operation on the lush Alaskan Island of Kodiak when Ken and Tanner buzzed her in Ken's Cessna 172 floatplane; they were on their way to a fishing trip and a photo shoot for a client.

Earlier that day, Angie unearthed a fist-size gold nugget. When she heard the plane overhead, she moved to a clearing and started jumping up and down while waving a bandana wildly in the air, motioning them to land.

"I think that she wants us to land," Tanner guessed.

"This better be good," Ken added.

They circled and landed on the river nearby. Angie met them on the beach where they landed.

All around the gold mining site where she was mining for the summer, there was a lot of earth moving and mining equipment, a D-8 dozer, a huge backhoe, a dump truck, a good-sized rock conveyer, gold dredges, a few generators, and a lot of odds and ends.

They walked into the command center tent, where four or five men were working with open maps spread on the tables. She walked them over to a five-foot safe inside a lockable wooden cabinet and pulled out a large coffee can, setting it on the table, revealing the seasons' findings.

"Check this out, boys," Angie said smugly as she showed them the nuggets.

"Holy cow. That is the biggest nugget I've ever seen," Ken exclaimed.

He turned to Angie and glanced at the men in the command center.

"Now that's what I'm talking about. Hawaii, here we come," Tanner said with excitement.

Angie's collection included a fist-sized nugget with about fifty other ½ thumb-size nuggets, a ½ inch of smaller nuggets, and gold dust.

"You are looking at over 1/2 a million for the season, and we still have a month to go," Angie stated.

"Woah," Tanner and Ken were amazed.

"Where were you guys heading when I pulled you out of the sky?" Angie asked as she pulled back the tent door flap on exiting.

"We were heading up the river to get some film footage and photos for a commercial we are putting together for a client," Tanner said as Angie and the guys stopped outside the tent to chat.

As they headed down the trail, the three of them rounded the corner of the lush vegetation revealing their plane on the beach fifty feet away, and to their surprise, they saw an 800-pound-brown-bear and her cub gathering berries.

Mama bear reared up, gave a death roar, and charged them; It was too late to run, and soon, the bear was all over Ken. After a few seconds of the brawl, Tanner pulled the sawed-off shotgun from the leg holster and blasted the bear, killing it.

But not before the bear landed a swipe on Ken’s face, almost taking out his eye and ripping a ten-inch 4- gash from his scalp downward across his face to his chin, almost ripping his face off.

Angie ran back to the camp, throwing open the tent door. Then, she grabbed the first-aid kit in a flash.

"A bear got Ken!" Angie yelled, panting.

She raced back, with four of her coworkers in hot pursuit.

When she got back, Tanner was cradling Ken.

Soon, they loaded Ken into the plane.

Luckily, one of the men at the command center called ahead and made sure that an ambulance was on the runway at the touch-down.

After a few hours, the doctor gave them the news. Ken was alive and well. He just had to keep his head fully wrapped and his leg alleviated and bandaged for a week or so.

Angie was shaken and felt guilty.

When speaking to Tanner while in the hospital waiting area, she said, "This would have never happened if I hadn't flagged you guys down."

"Now, sweetheart, don't try to blame yourself for this; it could have happened to any of us. We live in Alaska. This is the price we pay for living in the last frontier. This is one of the wildest and most dangerous places in the world to live." Tanner said, comforting her and trying to make her not be guilty about how the day unfolded.

"Thank God, we got him here as fast as we did. He could have died out there," he finished.

Chapter 11

Anchorage - First Encounter with Charlie

In the Alaskan metropolis of Anchorage, situated at the belly of the Cook Inlet, Tanner, Angie, and Ken had successfully found a decent apartment to rent.

That afternoon, while standing in the parking lot of the building, Tanner, Angie, and Ken were conversing with a new acquaintance they had recently crossed paths with. They discussed a possible lead on some gold mining equipment that they wanted to buy.

Their new acquaintance, Charlie, went inside his apartment, gave his connection a call, and discussed purchasing some mining equipment. He hung up and returned to the parking lot. With dismay, he said, “The guy said he already sold it.”

They walked inside the building and to Charlie’s apartment. Charlie settled on the couch and poured himself a drink. After taking a sip, he told Tanner, if you want to make some fast money, I have a friend sitting on five-thousand dollars’ worth of shrimp. And he only wants eight hundred dollars. It's worth five times that!"

"Sounds like a scam," Tanner said.

"It's for real!" answered Charlie. "He has kept it in a freezer on his shrimp boat."

Tanner asked, "Where can we talk to him?"

"You can't. He has it on his boat in Seward. All we would have to do is rent a truck, drive down, and give the money to the harbormaster. Pick it up, bring it back here and then sell it. And most of it has already been sold."

Tanner raised his eyebrow and questioned, "What's the catch?"

"There is none. He just wants to get back on the open sea," Charlie said. "He says they are having a big run this year."

The story wasn't convincing enough for Tanner.

He rubbed his temple and stated, "I don't know. It sounds fishy. Let us talk about it tonight. I'd like to discuss it with Angie and Ken, and then I'll give you a call tomorrow."

Charlie rolled his eyes, clearly not happy with how things were going.

"Tomorrow may be too late; it might be gone or spoken for by then," he said.

Tanner turned to Angie and asked, “What do you think, love? Feel like making some quick money?”

Angie replied, “Well, it sounds easy. My checking account could use a few extra bucks. Sure, why not?”

***

At Ryder truck rentals in Anchorage, while at the service counter, Charlie acted like he would be renting the truck until it came time to pay.

“Can you get this? I’m a little low on cash right now, but I’ll make it up to you when we sell the shrimp.”

When leaving, Charlie got in the driver’s seat of the truck. Tanner and Angie were sitting next to him, with Angie in the middle.

Charlie turned to them, smiled, and said, “This will be like taking candy from a baby.”

Tanner and Angie looked at each. They had a bad feeling about this encounter with Charlie.

The morning fog was still hovering close to the city streets when they pulled out of Anchorage that morning. The three barely engaged in any significant conversation for the rest of the journey.

Instead, Tanner and Angie’s hands were locked, their fingers interlaced between each other’s as they looked outside to the breathtaking view of the mountain range on the other side of the Turnagain arm as the bore tide rolled in. And of the lowland beside the highway that extended to the base of the Chugach Mountain range.

Driving down the Seward Highway and through Moose pass and bear creek, the truck approached Seward at the end of Resurrection Bay. They stopped at a bar when they got to Seward to grab a drink.

The three settled in the nightclub, which was very dark, except for the blue lights in some corners. Even the moonlight barely made past the small windows at the top of the nightclub.

Charlie was sitting alone on one side, and Angie and Tanner were on the other side of the table when a man approached and sat beside Charlie.

When they started to converse, the man introduced himself as a boat hand, and Charlie asked, “Are you from around here?”

The man shook his head and replied, “No. I’m just in town for a few days. Me and some buddies will be going to work for two months shrimping. We’re just looking for some cannabis before we go out on Monday.

Do you know anyone who has some for sale? We would like at least a pound, or maybe two. We have $1500 cash.”

Charlie set his drink on the table and said to the fisherman, "You know, I may just be able to help you out with that. Let me make a phone call."

***

Charlie stepped into the phone booth at the bar and dialed Rob's number. Charlie explained the situation to his connection.

Rob says, "Charlie. If you mess this up again, this will be the last time I will deal with you."

"Rob, I swear I'm trying to make things right. I'll call you when I get back into town."

Rob hung up, and Charlie returned to the table. He told the fisherman, "So when I get back tomorrow, I'll give you a call, and we can finish the deal."

"I see someone at the bar I need to talk to," Charlie excused himself and walked up to a guy at the end of the bar and had a few words with him.

The conversation heated up between the two. They got into a big scuffle, so the bouncer had to come over and step between them.

"Take it down the street, you guys?"

Danny, the man arguing with Charlie, said, pointing at him in vexation, "This guy owes me money, and he keeps jerking me around!"

"NOT MY PROBLEM!" the bouncer roared in a loud, intimidating voice.

Danny looked over to Charlie and said, "Let's step outside and deal with this."

"Uh...I have to get back to my friends," answered Charlie.

Danny smirked.

"Let me talk to your friends," he said, in his drunk, loud and disturbing voice. "They must not know you like I do."

Tanner and Angie were at the table, watching the whole scene unfold in shock. Just then, Charlie walked back to their table and apologized.

"Sorry. Just a little misunderstanding."

The next morning at the Stewart airport, Charlie was standing at the ticket counter, and the airline ticket lady said, "...And returning tomorrow at 9 p.m. Have a good trip, Mr. Dorsey."

When he settled in his seat, Charlie looked out the airplane window at the Chugach Mountains range in deep thought.

***

In the city of Wasilla, Alaska, when the plane landed that evening, Charlie taxied to Rob's estate.

When he entered the room, Rob was sitting on the sofa in the center of the room, and two thugs were sitting on either side, with Rob in the center.

Before Charlie could explain much, Rob ordered the two thugs. “Take him outside and rough him up. Then bring him back here.”

The thugs forced Charlie outside and punched and kicked him. Then, after a good beating, they brought him back to Rob’s office.

“Now, what’s this about you wanting some more product?” Rob asked.

Charlie, who was out of breath from the thug’s beating, held them by their arms and said breathlessly, “I met these guys in Seward who are going out on a fishing boat for three weeks on Monday.

They need some pot while they’re out. I need about two pounds of medium grade...”

“I’ll make sure you get all the money to help pay down my debt to you.”

Rob smirked, “Now that’s what I wanted to hear.”

Sighing, Charlie added, “I’ll have the $1500.00 to you by Tuesday.”

Rob gave the thugs a heads up, “Get him two pounds of the Mexican. I want $200.00 a pound, but you'll give me $1500.00 on

Tuesday. Or else, I'm going to break your legs. Is that the deal?"

Charlie was left with no other choice. He nodded, "That's the deal."

***

Back at the nightclub in Seward, Tanner and Angie enjoyed the evening to the fullest, drinking and laughing together.

"Well, it looks like we will be staying here for the evening. Might as well make the best of it. You want to dance?" suggested Tanner.

Angie said, "I love to, thought you'd never ask."

Tanner held her hand, and the two got up and headed for the dance floor.

As the two walked past the people at the club, Angie said, "That guy, Charlie, seems a little strange."

Tanner looked at her and said, "Let's just go along with him and see where it takes us."

Angie stopped in her tracks and said, "Okay, but we need to be extra cautious."

They got a hotel for the evening and picked up Charlie at the airport the next evening.

***

In the parking lot of Seward's local Grocery store the next day, Angie asked, "What are we doing?"

Charlie cleared his throat and said, "We need to pick up a few things for dinner. I'm going to cook us a meal that you won't soon forget. I need to get a few things for the boat too."

"Who is paying for this?" asked Tanner.

"Uh, I am. I have a little money. I will explain later," replied Charlie as they walked into the store.

Tanner, Angie, and Charlie rolled down the food aisle with a basket and a half full of groceries.

When they were done shopping, at the check-out counter, the checkout lady said, "That comes to $256.46."

Without hesitating or thinking for a second, Charlie wrote a check in a blink of an eye and handed it over to her.

This caught both Tanner and Angie by surprise, but the two remained silent, only passing each other a confused look.

Once outside the store, Tanner stopped Charlie and inquired, "Okay, what was that about?"

Charlie replied, "About two years ago, I got into a head-on accident on the Seward highway, up by Girdwood."

Angie pursed her lips, and Tanner said, "Do tell."

Charlie nodded and continued, “Some guy came over the center line on one of the curves. Just so happens we met, and he clipped me, spun me around, and it was a mess. But it could have been a lot worse.”

“I just talked to my lawyer. I should be getting my settlement money any day now.”

Angie and Tanner both looked at each other, and Tanner patted him on the back.

***

As the last rays of the sun disappeared beneath the horizon, they approached the harbor, stopped by the harbormaster's quarters, and gave the harbormaster the $800.00.

As they pulled onto the dock, there was a slight drizzle. The windshield wipers were flapping, and the headlights were glowing through the mist. They pulled up next to a 250’ shrimp vessel.

The three jumped onto the vessel, took off their coats as they went inside, and hung them in the coatroom.

After making the rounds in the vessel, back in the deck cabin now, Charlie said, “And this will be your cabin for the night.”

“Looks good,” Tanner said, and they left for the mess hall.

Sitting around the table eating a scrumptious meal, Tanner

told Charlie as he took a mouthful of a steak, “If we were in the old times, the king would have our heads if he knew we were eating like this without him.”

Charlie chuckled and then glanced at Angie’s plate and asked, “How do you like that lobster?”

“Incredible! But you know, I’ll have to get your recipe for this sauce,” said Angie.

Charlie raised his eyebrows and said, “No recipes given here.” He then pointed to his head and continued, “All my recipes are up here.”

Later in the darkness of the night, Tanner and Angie stood in the captain’s room, navigating their way in the shrimp boat. Coming to Charlie's room, the flashlight settled on the nightstand.

“Shaaaa! There it is,” Tanner said in a hushed voice.

He reached for it and opened the checkbook, sitting with Charlie’s keys and pocket change.

Tanner whispered to Angie, “Just as I thought.”

He flipped through the checkbook and saw $50,000 written on the starting balance, a few other entries, and then the one to the grocery store.

They had seen all they needed to see and made a quick exit out of the room.

Back at the deckhands' room, Angie said, "Just as we suspected, he's writing hot checks. I think this guy is not too trustworthy. Why didn't he just be honest with us?"

"He is just like a loose cannon, waiting to go off. I think he has a few ice cubes missing from the tray. We better keep a close eye on him," Tanner said.

***

When the sun rose, and the two woke up, Tanner and Angie started loading the shrimp into the back of the rented enclosed truck.

After about 45 minutes, with no help from Charlie, Tanner grumbled, "He has to be the laziest SOB I've ever met!"

Later that day, they hit the road back to Anchorage. As they approached the city, it was late in the evening. Inside the truck, the three of them could barely keep their eyes open.

"Tanner, I'm tired," Charlie said. "When we get to the apartments, I'm going right to bed, and I'll call you in the morning after I get a few hours of sleep. Then, when people are at work, we'll go out and sell the shrimp. Okay?"

Charlie dropped them off and went to park the truck, but Tanner had his suspicions. When they got to the apartment building, Tanner and Angie got out of the truck but went straight for their blazer.

Angie got into the driver's seat.

“This should be interesting,” she said to Tanner.

Soon after, they saw Charlie pulling away from the apartment complex with the shrimp.

Tanner blinked and said, “Let’s keep an eye on him; I don’t trust this guy.”

After following him for a while, Tanner said, “Looks like he’s pulling into that restaurant at the hotel. I bet he will sell the shrimp and keep the money.”

Chapter 12

More of Charlie

Tanner and Angie drove back to their apartment, careful not to raise any suspicions from Charlie about them following him to the restaurant.

When waking, the mid-morning sun shone brightly in the sky; still tired from the late night before, Tanner told Angie, "Best I talk to my friend on this."

Later that afternoon, Tanner called George, his biker friend.

"Hey, George, I need to talk to you about something," he said.

"Good to hear from you. What's up?" he asked.

Cutting straight to the chase, "It's all good except for one thing. Can you come over? I'll explain once you're here," Tanner said, and George agreed.

George, a rough-looking man with several scars on his face, was wearing a pair of black pants and a gray t-shirt, which barely covered the dragon tattoo on his left arm.

When entering the apartment, he asked in his husky tone, "So, what's the deal?"

Tanner suggested that they sit and talk, and he sat.

"I think we've got a situation here. I'm pretty sure someone is trying to rip me off…."

Tanner quickly explained how Charlie had tricked him and Angie and was possibly planning to hijack the shrimp, sell it and skip out on them with the money.

George, who was all ears to what Tanner told him, said, "I have a friend who has a moving van. But first, we need to find out where that shrimp is."

He thought and continued, "If we are going to turn the situation around and, in our favor, we need to get a jump on it. We have to set up a sting."

"Do you have other friends who can help us with this?" George asked.

"I might have one. Ross. What are you thinking?" Tanner asked.

"Perfect. Give the man a call and see if he can help us out."

Tanner called Ross immediately.

"Hey, Ross. How are you doing?"

“I am good, Tanner. What about you?” he said.

“Good, good. I would really appreciate your help if you've got some time.”

“What’s up?” he asked.

Tanner explained the situation.

Ross replied, “I’ll call around and see if I can locate the shrimp.”

“That’ll be a great help.”

“Tanner, I’ll get on it right away. Once I locate the shrimp, which shouldn’t take very long, I will give you a call, and then we’ll figure out what to do next.”

Tanner thanked him, hung up, called George, and told him that Ross was all in and he was calling around to try to locate the shrimp.

***

That afternoon Ross called back.

“I have good news,” he said. “I located the shrimp.”

“Seriously?!” Tanner said incredulously.

“Yeah. It wasn’t hard. The owner said Charlie told him he would be back for it tomorrow.”

Tanner quickly got on the phone and told George that the shrimps had been located and Charlie would be back for it tomorrow.

"Perfect!" George said. "Now we have got to figure out the sting, how we are going get that shrimp back, and how to throw Charlie off track without him suspecting anything, a detour."

The two sat together, discussing plans for the detour and laying out a perfect course of action without any loopholes. As they did so, the cups of coffee kept increasing on the side table. As the minutes ticked by, they finally agreed upon a plan.

Tanner called Ross and updated him on the plan.

"I've been trying to get in touch with Charlie. I called him three times and got no answer," Tanner stated. "Now, it's time to put the plan into action."

A few hours later, Tanner finally connected with Charlie.

"I have someone who wants to buy two pounds of Thai weed. He will be at my house tonight at 7:00 pm. Can you get a hold of some?" Tanner asked.

After a moment's silence, Charlie answered, "Okay. Let me reach out to my connection in the business. But I think all he has in that class is Matanuska Purple."

"Mata... what?" asked Tanner; he had never heard of that.

Charlie laughed and said, “Matanuska purple is its name. And believe me, it will blow your mind!”

“Alright. Get in touch with him and let me know if we can get it delivered tonight,” Tanner said and ended the call.

A few minutes later, Tanner’s phone started to ring. It was Charlie calling.

“I was right. All he has is the Matanuska purple. I hope that’s going to be all right?” Charlie asked.

Tanner told him to hold on while he pretended to ask his friends if Matanuska purple was alright.

“They said that would be fine. We’ll be waiting for you, with cash in hand.”

Charlie answered, “Perfect,” with a hint of excitement, not suspecting that the situation was about to change.

“Well then, it’s all set,” Charlie continued. “We will be there at seven. I’m bringing two guys, and we’ll have two pounds. He wants $2,000 a pound.”

“We’ll be waiting,” Tanner said and hung the phone up.

At 7:00, a knock came on the door. Tanner couldn’t help but glance at his watch.

“Right on time,” he said to the others. “Franky, go to the

kitchen and act like nothing's happening. George, you are the money man."

George sat on the Easy Boy recliner, looking through the newspaper. He took his gun and put it under the newspaper. When he gave Tanner a heads up, Tanner opened the door.

Ross and Frankie were acting cool in the front area of Tanner's apartment, waiting for Charlie to walk in.

Tanner and Frankie welcomed Charlie and his two friends. One of them was carrying a shopping bag. Frankie checked the pot and its content as they walked into the back room.

Tanner stopped Charlie and said, "We know what you are trying to do. You are not ripping us off. You are playing with our man's money, and he doesn't like the way things have been going down lately."

Charlie's face turned pale, and he moved his lips to say something, but Tanner cut him off.

"He would like to talk to you."

With a lump in his throat, Charlie followed Tanner into the living room where George was sitting.

When Charlie stood in front of him, George revealed the gun and then pulled the gun's hammer while targeting Charlie.

"My friend tells me you are trying to pull a fast one on him and that you owe him about four thousand dollars for his time and money. Well, part of that money is mine," George said in his commanding, husky tone.

He gave Charlie a death stare, breaking Charlie's train of thought, and continued, "If I were you, I would get out of here while you're still able to."

Charlie and his two accomplices scrambled for the door with eyes and mouths wide open, gasping for air. But before Charlie made his way out of the apartment, he turned to Tanner.

Mad as hell while gritting his teeth, "I'm going to get you, Tanner. If it is the last thing I ever do," Charlie said.

***

That night, $4,000 worth of high-grade cannabis was laid out across the bed in Tanner's bedroom. As he shoved his clothes inside his medium-sized suitcase, he wrapped the pot in a t-shirt and carefully hid it between his clothes.

Angie packed a few belongings and everything of value from Tanner's apartment in a hurry and loaded them into the blazer.

Tanner shut the blazer's door and got into the driving seat.

"Where to now, my love?" Angie asked.

Tanner started the blazer and hit the accelerator, saying, "I have a friend in Hawaii I've been meaning to visit for a while now."

Early next morning, Ross drove them to the airport.

Midmorning, the plane touched down on a different runway. As the passengers were ready to deboard the plane, the captains announced through the intercom, *"Thank you for trusting Coastal Air for your travels. We hope you enjoy your stay in Hawaii."*

"I can't believe it. Just this morning, we were in Alaska, and now we are in Hawaii," Angie said as she peeped out the window, smiling.

Chapter 13

What Makes the World Go Around

Later that day, Tanner was visiting his old friend on the Island of Kauai, Hawaii. A reunion was long overdue, and what better time than this, when they were both far from their California homes.

On the terrace at Hugh's apartment, the mid-morning sun rose high in the sky, and the friends chatted for hours. The most celebrated amongst those were Tanner's Alaskan adventures. An adventure, the essence of which in some sense was yet to pay off for Tanner.

Sipping a cup of coffee, Hugh said, "One day, I was floating in a river with a friend of mine. And, we had this good intel that told my partner and me that we'd find gold in those California hills.

After floating the river for almost a day, we were close to calling it a day.

Just before we signed off, my friend caught sight of a shiny object next to a pebble. We thought it was an aluminum can pull tab at first. But it turned out to be a nice size nugget. By the end of the day, we had a quarter of a coffee can filled with gold."

He sighed and continued, "We were so happy, we felt like a puppy with ten tails, but it was short-lived by a couple of pirates in black wet suits.

They said they were military police. The fuckers held us at gunpoint and took all the gold we had spent hours collecting, saying we were trespassing on government property."

Tanner chuckled and poked fun at him, saying, "And I'm supposed to believe that luckless fairytale?"

Hugh rolled his eyes in dismay and replied, "You can believe whatever you want to. But I'm here to tell you that there is gold in those hills right there. If only you're willing to put in the effort to make it happen, it can be yours."

Tanner raised his eyebrows and derided, "Yeah, and then some jerk comes by and takes it from us, and all our efforts go down the drain?"

"Or because our government wants to extort 50 grand from a law-abiding family or some nonsense like that. Maybe the man has a monkey on his back, and he ends up dead."

"No thanks, I'm glad to be happy and free with a good woman, and *no one behind*, no one breathing down my neck," he took a breath.

Hugh cocked his head sideways and said, “Bro! You need to live a little. You could get hit by a car today or next week. Tomorrow is not guaranteed.

You never know when your time is up. The next thing you know, you'll find yourself pushing up daisies, surrounded by bugs. Adventure awaits us all while we wait for that fateful day.”

“No thanks, but maybe, I’ve always thought a little gold mining would be fun,” Tanner continued, “I get my thrills, my adrenaline pumping, by hanging off cliffs. You have no idea, my friend, what it’s like to be 1000 feet up on the side of a rock, overlooking a gorgeous valley, the green canopy of trees, the water trickling down the side of the cliff, being part of the elements of nature. It's like flying and seeing the world from up above, a different perspective altogether. I wouldn't mind dying right there. My life would be complete. That is what I call heaven. My heaven.”

Hugh took another sip from his mug and responded, “Ok, since we're on the subject, what do you think about religion?”

Tanner scoffed at the question.

“What do you mean what do I think about it?” he asked. “A Man’s religion or God’s religion? Because, personally, I'd say I think we are the aliens that we have been looking for all these years. No need to look for aliens on Mars or wherever. We’re right here!”

Hugh put down his coffee cup on the table and looked perplexed.

'*What in the world is he saying?*' he thought.

Tanner smiled and continued, "See, here's my theory. I believe we are a planet from a planet of beings that are light years ahead of us. Maybe, who knows for sure.

For argument's sake, say, over six thousand years ago, a spacecraft landed on earth filled with aliens and mated with our woman. We have blended into their past pretty well, wouldn't you say. Just a thought."

Tanner was being silly, but Hugh was not taking Tanner's words lightly.

"Back up, so what do you mean? That there a difference between God's religion and a man's?" Hugh questioned.

Tanner rubbed his temple and then clarified, "Oh. Yeah, totally. See, man destroys everything he gets his hands on. Look at our food, for example.

But the fact is that we are still a young world, and we make the futures we want for our nations and lives."

He stopped for a moment and then questioned Hugh.

"Answer me this. What is time? And where do you think it came from?"

“Tell me. What is it?” Hugh asked.

Tanner smiled and answered, “It is the unwanted byproduct of energy and lives in man's mind.”

“I can't tell you for sure if God exists or not, but I do know that there are benefits to living a Godly life. I don't believe there is a great big man somewhere up there, with a big stick just waiting to whack us if we do something bad. Or that we will burn in hell for eternity for being born in this back assward society.

I believe that living with the thought that there is a God to whom we are accountable for the things we do, all our actions and deeds does give a person pause and purpose,” he continued.

“I don't believe in all the Bible, in its entirety, but I believe it was written by wise men with great moral compasses. And that they were right for their time.”

Tanner then explained, “I hear the stories in the Bible, and I'd say they are great stories. So are, and will always be. But I wasn't there. There is so much room for speculation, but they are good life lessons.

But the bottom line for me is that they are not personal. God is not doing his job if He loses my soul because he has not worked His love in my life and made Himself so real that I see Him everywhere I look.

Personally, I see His creative powers in nature, mountains, trees, humanity."

"I look up in the night sky and think about how big the universe is. And then I look downward at the smaller things around us. I think about the minuscule atoms, invisible to the naked eye. And then I think of how we are the universe's grand creation, and everything is meaningless without humanity and consciousness.

God permeates the universe and is the universe. God is that big of a universal spirit, and at the same time, He lives in man's heart. He changes people's lives and mends broken people. We are a part of his universe, and so we are his beings. We are his limbs and his mouthpiece in a sense."

Tanner's smile widened, and his face lit up. He continued, "Or... are we just a grand experiment from an advanced civilization, light years ahead of us? No one knows for sure.

I do know this, though; nothing means anything without man's comprehension. And where did man's comprehension come from, or how did the eye evolve from nothing? There are so many questions."

He then pinned Hugh with a question, "And then there is Jesus. What do you do with Jesus?"

Hugh, who had completely been baffled by all this

conversation, responded only by passing a confused shrug.

Tanner went on with his theory, "You see, in the Bible, there are seventy-one specific predictions of when and how Jesus would come.

It's been said that the likelihood of that happening to one man at this specific time in man's history is a trillion to one. Or like if you filled the state of Texas up, knee-high, with silver dollars, and painted one red, and then blindfolded a person and asked them to pick the red out. What I'm getting at is that it's very improbable."

Tanner's forehead wrinkled, and he continued, "It is man who makes salvation much harder than God's own plan for everlasting life. As far as I can tell, this is nothing but God's proving ground, an experiment to see if we can handle everlasting life or not."

***

Angie was working as a teacher in the city of Fairbanks, Alaska, Alaska's largest city and, by far, the coldest among the other cities in the interior. The home of the University of Alaska Fairbanks, which boasts of being the founding campus of the University of Alaska campuses, had proved to be a welcoming place for them to make a home for a while.

At this prestigious and renowned University, Angie was teaching a class in gold studies where her students were designing an exhibit of the Klondike Gold Rush of Chilkoot Pass in 1898, which connected Alaska with British Columbia in Canada.

A 4x8 sheet of plywood, placed in front of them on a lab table with a paper-mache replica of the mountains and golden staircase, and the thirty-three-mile trek which the stampeders had, in those days, taken to get to the gold fields in Dawson, Canada from the Dyea valley in the United States.

Angie addressed the students seated in the class. She said, "The sad part about it is that many stampeders spent thousands of dollars. In fact, many spent all they had in the whole world to get to the gold fields, only to find that most of the mines had already been staked out and that there was very little gold left behind for them to take back home."

Angie pointed to Skagway on the exhibit and said, "After graduating from college, I spent a summer working there, as a dance hall girl, in the tourist action Soapy Smith and his dance hall girls."

She told them of her experiences there and the adventure she undertook with Tanner when he arrived there the next summer.

***

Rolling down the highway, Tanner hit the accelerator. The sun was high in the sky but not sharing much of its heat yet. It was still early in the summer. He was on his way to talk to some of his hiking buddies about where they were planning on going for their next climb. Suddenly, he caught sight of two of his old buddies at a gas station. So, he switched to reverse gear and pulled up next to them.

He got out of his truck, fist drawn, acting like they were in trouble. But they knew he was a jokester.

They were all geared up for a hang-glider outing.

Pinto, one of his old friends with long brunette hair flowing in the wind, said, “Hey Tanner, how the heck have you been? It’s been quite a while, bud. So what have you been up to these days?”

Tanner gave him a fist bump and replied, “Just doing some climbing. And you know I opened a photo studio in town. Right!”

In a quizzical tone, Pinto said, “Yeah? I heard a little something about that. What's the name?”

“Studio 1220,” replied Tanner. “It’s out on the Northern lights’ boulevard And Davidson. You ought to stop by and check it out.”

“I will, in the next few days. Maybe we can work together. I have some ideas for the photos I’ve been taking. I’d like to turn them into a slide show and put some rock and roll music in it," Pinto said enthusiastically.

"That'd be cool. I look forward to seeing you," replied Tanner. "Where are you going now?"

Pinto walked to the back side of his truck, showing him the glider he was sporting, "Just picked up a new toy. It's a new thing. It's called a hang glider. I just had to have one. It's only my third time out, but it's like flying like a bird. I just love it."

He touched its king post and continued, "My buddy, Art, found a nice place he wants to try. We're heading there now."

***

Outside Tanner's solar-powered cabin, in the low mountains of Fairbanks, on the dust-covered, washed-out road, stood two men in complete trekking gear with backpacks on their shoulders. Pinto and Chris were part of their close group of friends.

They knocked on the door several times but received no answer even though Tanner's blazer and Angie's car were parked in the drive. Finally, after looking through the front window, Pinto and Chris let themselves in. Determining from the two cups on the coffee table that Tanner and Angie must be home.

Pinto pushed open the front door and walked in.

He said, "I don't think they will mind if we let ourselves

in. After all, they are expecting us."

Chris nodded and answered, "They must be somewhere on the property. After all, it is the best part of the morning, and the Alaskan sun is burning bright."

As the two strolled through the cabin, looking for Angie and Tanner, they heard a commotion coming from the backroom. Following the noise, Pinto and Chris headed to the back. On the way, Chris grabbed a cup of coffee and a Rock-climbing magazine that Tanner had sitting on the coffee table.

Tanner and Angie were in the backroom with their camping and hiking gear spread out on the floor. In the magazine Chris picked up, there was an article about the Legend of lost gold.

Things were about to get real.

***

With the fire lit up at the campsite under the vast blanket of the sky and the crescent moon smiling at them, Tanner walked over with some supplies in his hand.

He said, "Time is money. I need you guys to look alive and lock down this operation. We are going to need all hands on deck."

Ken had come over on a four-wheeler with a box-bed on the back, towing a trailer to haul the gold out.

"As soon as we can, let's load up the gold and get out of

here," Ken said.

While warming his hands, Pinto asked, "Is there enough fuel to get us down the mountain?"

Ken smirked, saying, "You are talking to the king of fuel. There is enough fuel to run a small city for a week, buddy."

He winked.

Just as he did so, Pinto noticed Ken's scar. He glared at it in horror and said, "Boy, that is nasty!"

"Talk about ruining a good day. That bear almost killed me. But, when we get that money under our belts, this scar is history," Ken said.

"How much do you think we'll get to keep?" asked Pinto.

"About 60% is what Tanner was told," Ken said. "But we'll see."

With a smile on his face, Ken sighed, "That's not too bad. I hope they keep their word, though."

"It's the government, so who knows?" said Ken.

Chapter 14

The Gold Recovery and Last Encounter with Charlie

A couple of days had passed since they set up their base camp at Wrangell-St. Elias Mt., Tanner, and his three climbing buddies, Ken, Michael, and Pinto, were forced to stay back, postponing their trek. The fierce winds had blown their camp tent way down the mountain a couple of times.

Tired and frustrated, Tanner and the crew started to set up another base camp.

Although the operation was meant to be lowkey, they hadn't imagined it would take so long. And the tough grind of it was never on their cards.

Twice they had started the trek up the mountain. Twice, they were sent back by the howling winds. But that's the thing about these climbs; you can never really know what's waiting for you on mountain expeditions like these.

By dusk, they were done safely securing the tent in place. Then they put together a small campfire to take the chill off their bones.

As the darkness built a stronghold around them, stars glistened in the night, but no moon came to greet them. Tanner and his partners shared a small meal together in the coziness of the four-man tent at the camp and dozed off.

In the twilight of the next morning, waiting for the sun to rise over the horizon, they were praying in their own heads that they could fight and win the odds of the intense winds giving them more problems and move ahead this time.

***

As the dawn approached, the sun rays were landing hard on the side of the tent. Lighting Tanner's face, he rubbed his eyes and woke up. He looked over at Ken. Ken was awake but in his own world. "Ken! Wake up. It's getting late. We're burning daylight!

Wake up, my friend."

Tanner shook him, and Ken opened his eyes.

"Oh, God! Is it already time? I just fell asleep."

"Get up. You can tell me about your dreams later," Tanner said.

They quickly broke down the camp, loaded their backpacks, ate breakfast, and started up the mountain. It was a glorious morning. It seemed that the mountain was going to give them a break today.

A couple of hours into their climb, the winds started to pick up again, wavering them off their balance. The visibility was close to none at that point.

Ken looked at Tanner with Michael and Pinto in line through steamed goggles and asked, "Shall we continue or rest for a while? I need to pee."

"Do your thing. I'm not going anywhere."

Tanner stopped and looked up at the sky. The sky was thick with slightly blowing white clouds engulfing them. He took a deep breath and said, "I don't see any signs of real threatening clouds. I think this won't be that bad. Let's keep moving."

Ken shook his business.

He trusted Tanner's judgment.

At one point, almost four hours later, near the mountain ridge, the winds were so bad that some of their climbing gear blew half a mile down the hill. They held each other's arms for support and looked behind at their rolling gear.

Slowly, they took steps ahead, trying their best to find a safer spot to rest a while. Ken pulled a pick-ax from the loop on his snow pants. The snow was turning to ice cliffs.

"You guys stay back. Me and Ken are going around the bend to see what it looks like up ahead." Tanner screamed into the winds.

A few minutes into their exploratory trek, Tanner, pointed

as the wind tore at his close and ice was caking his goggles. He focused on the point and said, “Are those tracks? I’m getting the feeling that someone is following us.” The wind kept howling, “I bet Charlie is on the mountain.”

“I get that feeling too,” screamed Ken.

They traversed to the area where they spotted the tracks, which started to get steep. So steep that their shoulders were now touching the mountainside. They stared wide-eyed as the realization struck them that what they thought to be tracked in the snow were actually snowballs rolling down the mountain.

Ken exclaimed, “I am not ready for this.”

Tanner was spellbound. He looked around and finally spotted Charlie with his goons.

The three of them were on the ridge below them. Tanner informed Ken about them as they stepped aside, trying to hide from Charlie and his thugs.

“Let’s get back to the camp. We need to find and lay claim to the gold before Charlie,” Tanner said.

Just then, Tanner’s foot slipped on the ice rock he was standing on and grabbed onto Ken in haste to save himself from falling off the mountain and into a 500-foot snow shoot to certain death.

In an instant, both of them were sliding down the

mountainside, tumbling as the snow was sliding with them. They got about three hundred feet into their slide and dropped into a snow-covered cavern.

Down below, Charlie looked up and saw the commotion. He heard the yells from Ken and Tanner as they were sliding down the mountainside, then he saw them disappear.

After a few moments of being stunned and confused, Tanner and Ken regained their wits, breath, and orientation.

Tanner brushed off the snow and grime from his gear pack and said, "What the hell just happened?"

"We must have just died," Ken said as he sighed. It was pitch black except for a stream of light that was coming in the hole they fell through,

A blank stare came on Tanner's face, and he said, "No, because I'm right here, and you're right there."

"Look, that must be the pearly gates," Ken pointed to an old, rusted plane that came to view when he lit a warning flare that lit up the old mining cave.

Tanner grappled and struggled. He then moved some dirt clumps inside the cavern, blocking his view.

"Is that what I think it is?"

•••

Tanner and Ken had stopped by a local food/gas station to top off the gas tank for the journey ahead. This hip town, McCarthy, AK, was commonly referred to as the climber's takeoff point.

"Angie? Honey, how are you?" Tanner asked Angie. She seemed agitated. It had been almost a week since he had last contacted her.

"How have I been? Missing you since you left," she said.

"Sweetness, we'll be back soon. But guess what? WE FOUND THE GOLD."

Angie paused in her anger, "What?! Are you serious?"

"Sweetness. You will not believe how we stumbled on to it!" Tanner said, beaming through the phone.

Beside him was an old man about 84 years old, sitting in a rocking chair, passing the time.

Tanner cleared his throat and said, "I'll tell you all about it later today. But for now, I just wanted to let you know that we're safe. Call my dad and tell him we found and touched the gold. It's safe, but we must work on the recovery plan fast."

"I'll get right on it," Angie replied.

Tanner added, "And babe, I love you."

He ended the call and walked out of the booth.

"Excuse me, sir. Are you from around here?" Tanner asked the old man napping in a rocking chair as he came out of the phone booth. The town still had old wooden sidewalks from a time in the past when the town was booming.

"Yeah, I grew up in these parts," he replied. "Who's asking," the old man asked with a stern look on his face.

"I'm just toying with you, son," a warm smile settled on his face. "Seen a lot of stuff in my time. When I was a kid, we used to find copper under these wooden sidewalks.

"What brings you to our fine little town?" asked the old man.

"I hear there's some gold in these here hills, and I aim to find it," Tanner commanded.

With the old man's gaze pinned at Tanner as though studying his abilities, he said, "A lot of people have tried. And a lot of people have… died."

Tanner swallowed hard and asked, "Is that so? Do tell."

"Well, you see, I've been combing these hills for forty years," the old man said. "And the outcome - a lot of cold, wasted years."

Tanner bit his lip and said, "What if I told you, you can't get to it unless you're a serious rock climber?"

Raising an eyebrow, the old man said, “Do you know something I don’t?”

“NO, NO. I’m just saying.” Tanner tried to walk back his statement.

“I think you might like to meet my grandson,” said the old man. “I feel like you have a lot in common. He’s a rock climber too.”

***

Chad, a twenty-six-year-old rock climber about fifteen years younger than Tanner, strutted into the kitchen of his grandpa’s cabin.

“My Grandpa says, you say you found the gold?!” Tanner’s real reason for coming to town had been exposed.

With a smile spread on his face, Tanner replied, “True, and I need to put together a climbing team as soon as possible.”

“Perfect! I love a good Recovery,” Chad said. “I’m studying to be a medic at UCLA and don’t need to be back until the middle of Jan. And I have a lot of good connections in LA who would love to document the find.”

Tanner was cool, “Cool, my wife is a professor at University in Fairbanks and holds a degree in geology. She’s currently teaching her students gold recovery techniques.”

"I must warn you, though," Tanner said, his tone as serious as ever. "A winter climb and recovery will not be a picnic. Are you really up for it?"

"Are you kidding? I've climbed this mountain 4 times in the winter. So I know that mountain like the back of my head," Chad said and smiled.

Tanner laughed and said, "OK then, we're going to get along just fine. But I need to tell you. It could get nasty. I have someone on my trail. Let's say he is determined to make my life a hell."

"But we'll deal with him when we have to," Tanner said with a smirk on his face.

Chad gave him a fist bump and said, "Ok then."

It reminded Tanner of his dad.

"Do you happen to have a phone I can use? I need to call my dad, the money man," Tanner asked.

Chad pointed to the phone on the desk.

***

Tanner's dad was sitting at his office desk when the phone started to ring.

He picked up the phone. "Hello? Don McKenzie here,"

"Dad, it's me,"

Don's face lit up, "God, I've been waiting to hear from you for days. Are you alright?"

"Yes, dad. I'm fine, but we need to act fast," Tanner said.

Don replied, "I got a call from Angie, she didn't tell me much, but she did say that you're okay, you found the gold, and that we need to work fast. I'm on it. Call this Number. Jacques is up to date and waiting to hear from you."

"I'm on my way back to the site," Tanner said. "I've put together a climbing team.

Angie is in charge of the ground operations and communications."

"I wish you God's speed, and for goodness' sake, be careful son," Don said.

***

An encounter at the rescue site with Charlie and his thugs was coming.

The moon was shining bright when Tanner, his climbing team, Charlie, and his thugs came head-to-head, and the bloody encounter broke out.

Charlie and his two thugs entered the cavern unnoticed, with guns drawn and them ducking undercover.

Charlie saw Tanner loading gold bars into the back of the 4-wheeler and fired a shot. Fortunately, it missed but startled him, and he took cover.

One of Charlie's goons snuck around to the other side of the plane.

Ken, who remained unnoticed until then, jumped out, giving a spiral kick to the thug, and knocked the gun from his hand. With another kick across the face, Ken knocked him out cold and put a bullet through the back of his head.

Now, Ken had two guns.

Ken took cover in the cockpit. Bullets were piercing the cool night's air.

One of the thugs lit a stick of dynamite and was getting ready to throw it when one of Tanner's team, Chad, snatched it from his hand, and a fight ensued.

The dynamite fell to the ground.

A beat later, the thug saw someone snuff out the dynamite.

The thug glanced up and saw a gun barrel. Ken pulled the trigger, and his lights went out.

***

The plane's rear loading door was rusted and severely

damaged, revealing crates of wartime supplies and gold.

Charlie took cover behind a crate of wool blankets while Tanner grabbed onto an overhead pulley, on what once was a rolling track, the sounds of the bullets filling the air went silent.

Tanner caught Charlie by surprise and kicked a gun from Charlie's hand as he dropped in close.

Charlie grabbed a rusted metal cinching rod and swung it at Tanner. Tanner jumped back, just barely avoiding a swipe to the head and what would have surely put him out of business.

Tanner lunged himself at Charlie, giving him a body-hug and a chokehold. Charlie fought hard and broke loose.

He took hold of the rod again and took a few more swipes at Tanner, landing one in his gut. Tanner bellied over but returned with a fist to Charlie's face; Charlie spun around.

They tussled some more, and Tanner threw a few rapid-fire blows at Charlie's face.

Tanner saw that Charlie pulled out another gun from the back of his pants, and he kicked it away.

Suddenly, they found themselves entangled in the piles of blankets that had slowly deteriorated over the years.

Charlie looked up with a bloody face. Signs of defeat were written all over his battered body. Suddenly, a bullet entered his body from nowhere, and he went limp.

***

Minutes later, darkness spread its shadow onto them, and his vision became nil. Tanner coughed blood and closed his eyes.

Out of the blue, sirens hit his eardrums. He saw a few men through the misty vision. Unrecognizable, they barged into the cavern.

“Tanner?” heard one say. “Your dad sent us and said we would find you here.”

They were there to ensure he and his expedition comrades returned safely home and that the gold was being properly looked after.

Tanner could hold on no more and passed out.

The rescue team loaded the three dead climbers into body bags, and onto the helicopter, along with Tanner.

His buddies and team secured the gold bars on the back of the four-wheeler trailer and took them off the mountain.

And this is where we start the prelude to the story (chapter Zero).

Three months after Tanner's 41st birthday and time in the hospital, a special national event had been planned and was now taking place.

***

With the gold worth sixty-five million successfully extracted, sixty percent, as was promised by the government, was to be distributed to Tanner and his team. That accounted for their portion of the gold worth a cool thirty-nine million.

The host made the announcement as the stands of the baseball stadium roared high. People had poured into the stadium—about a million gold hunters, waiting to hear the celebrated names of those who had successfully found the treasure.

The compere made the announcement, and the crowd cheered.

"Tanner McKenzie, from Burlingame, California. Aged 41, a professional photographer, Rock climber, and all-around good person. The Expedition Head, receiving 40% of the take, i.e., $15,600,000."

Tanner walked up to the stage, and his team followed as their names were being called out.

"Angie, from Sonora, California. Mr. McKenzie's wife. She's a professor at Alaska University, Fairbanks, holding degrees in geology: gold studies. And the head of ground operations, receiving 20% of the take, i.e., $7,800,000."

Ken, Pinto, and Chad each received 13% of the take, which was $5,070,000 per head. With 1% going toward supplies, travel, food, and services.

Tanner was invited to address the crowd.

He walked to the podium and said, "I want to thank my dad for lighting the spark in me as a child. Then, to be an adventurer, to go out on my own and explore this great country that we live in. Countless men and women have given their lives and everything they had so that we could live as free people. I think of World War I and World War II and how we've evolved as a nation. And I am so proud to be part of the greatest nation on Earth and that the world has ever known.

But I need to tell you that we need to be diligent and protect our unique way of life because we are the envy of the world. And we might think that we are in the clear, but we all know that things can change in the blink of an eye. The freedoms we hold dear today can be a memory tomorrow."

The crowd roared.

"We are a baby nation, capable of great things," Tanner continued. "I want to share a couple of things I have learned on my walk through life. One is that we can direct this journey of life. And the other is that people usually get what they deserve. That may sound mean, but it's true. So, make your choices with much reflection and wisely. The universe bends to man's heart, so keep your heart in tune with the universe.

***

A Ticker Parade was organized in New York a couple of weeks later. Millions of people lined the streets with balloons and confetti everywhere. Tanner, Angie, Ken, Pinto, and Chad were sitting and waving to the Crowd from the back seat of a convertible '42' Dodge Power Wagon personal carrier. It looked like a blazer or modern-day Tahoe. It had four windows in the back that could be rolled up and down and had a cloth top that could be removed, sitting on raised one-ton axles, with dualies on the back. It was sporting a gold army star on both doors, with a beautiful forest green paint job.

It was a beautifully restored one used in WW11. The same year the cargo plane with the gold went missing. When the generals were paraded through wartime camps, they would stand up and wave to the soldiers.

Now it was Tanner, Angie, and the team's turn. They stood up and waved to the crowds lining the streets of Manhattan Boulevard in You Nork City, USA.

Tanner turned to look at Angie and said, "The world makes sense again. I think we're going to be okay!"

Angie pinched his cheeks and smiled, "You're a funny guy! But I love you anyway."

THE END

POSTLUDE TO THE ADVENTURE – Remember, if you enjoyed this story and had fun immersing yourself in the adventure, get this book in the hands of your favorite Netflix, Amazon, or another big-time producer with a 10 million dollar+ budget or big-time acter with connections, it will take a lot of resources to turn this adventure into a blockbuster of a movie.

Try to set up a meeting, and if we make a deal, I'll do you right with a 10% finder's fee.

Made in the USA
Las Vegas, NV
20 October 2023

79390934R00085